D1733320

Uniformly
Undeserved
P. Scott Corbett

Dapshow Publications

DAPSHOW
PUBLICATIONS

1

    Morio Takara and his best friend Rin Kineshiro stood outside the gate to their compound and looked with a bit of self-satisfaction at their work. They had rather artfully used leaves to spread the cow's blood on the walls, the portal, and the gate entering their little community. It was fresh and therefore still bright red. As they looked through the entrance, they could see the bold swaths of reddish-brown blood they had smeared on the walls of the buildings inside. Turning around and looking towards the pathway that led away from their sanctuary, they were satisfied that the straw rope with bones affixed, and dangling down was hung on the low branches of the trees across and on both sides of the passage to their home to ward off evil.

    It was 1903 and as Okinawans had begun to adopt the Japanese superstition that three was a lucky number, there was optimism that it would be a good year. At sixteen, both Morio and Rin were delighted to be recruited to participate in the preparation for the annual Shimakusarashi purification festival that their little community celebrated every February. They had reached the age of fuller participation in more than just the productive labor of their little hamlet but also its spiritual life. They could smell the cow's heart being boiled in preparation for its presentation at Seifa Utaki, the sacred place, not far into the hills on the backside of their compound. Tradition held that was where the goddess Amamikyu came down to earth and gave birth to the Okinawans. After presenting some of the heart at Seifa Utaki, the remaining cow's meat would be distributed to all as part of a glorious feast.

"Are you ready to go?" Morio's father, Ono asked smiling as he approached. "Here, you carry the special jug to collect some of the water at the Seifa Utaki well." Morio was proud to be entrusted with the task.

"Be careful with it, don't drop it. There would be a torrent of tribulation for us all if you did," Ono warned.

"Don't worry Father, it is safe with me," Morio assured.

And so, they set off up the hill towards Seifa Utaki with Morio's father carrying some carefully wrapped cow's heart in a backpack and Morio with the family heirloom jug. They walked at a comfortable pace and Ono hummed some traditional tunes quietly and smoked his customary pipe and purple tobacco as they walked.

"Try not to make too much noise dear boy," Ono cautioned Morio. "We must always be happy to enjoy the luxury of just enjoying nature."

As they neared Seifa Utaki, Ono turned to Morio. "How you doing, son? I noticed you had a pretty big bowl of tea while you and Rin were painting the blood. If you need to go, you better do it here because we don't want to desecrate the shrine with any of your urine."

Though Morio thought he could hold it, he had no idea how long they would be at the Utaki. So, he excused himself and wound his way into the forest of trees in order to attend to his business.

Meanwhile, Ono continued a bit further towards the shrine. But suddenly Morio could hear the crashing sound of someone clumsily going in the direction of his father and the shrine. The intruder seemed nearly out of breath. Morio began to quickly finish his business to go and investigate.

"Hey, you," a man in a Japanese police uniform called out to Ono. "Where are you going and what do you think you are doing?"

Ono turned around and fixed a disapproving gaze on the man. With a minimum amount of politeness, he responded: "Excuse me?"

3

"You heard me, you Okinawan bugger. What are you doing here?"

Trying to abbreviate their conversation and confrontation, Ono answered: "It is the custom of my people and clan to come and visit Seifa Utaki to honor the sacred spirits and appeal for good fortune, especially during the Shimakusarashi festival."

"What's that you have slung on your back?" the policeman demanded.

"It is some boiled cow's heart as an offering to Amamikyu."

"You mean our Japanese sun goddess Amaterasu-Ōmikami?" the obviously inebriated policeman, said correcting Ono.

"No, I mean Amamikyu our Okinawan creation goddess."

"Ah, balderdash. You foolish Okinawans are all muddled about the gods and spirits," he said approaching Ono in an aggressive manner. "You are all basically barbarians."

"And you Japanese harriers are so ignorant of anyone but yourselves and have no respect for other people's beliefs."

At that, the policeman advanced on Ono and struck him with his walking stick. Ono recoiled backwards to ward off blows, stumbled and fell to the ground at the policeman's mercy. The crocked constable stood over Ono and began to raise his riding crop.

Morio saw his father's danger as he approached the encounter. He ran as fast as he could and tackled the policeman from behind taking him to the ground. They began to grapple, and the policeman tried to roll off his stomach to defend himself. Morio was big for his age and strong from all the hard fieldwork he had been doing for years. He grabbed the policeman in a bear hug and holding on to the policeman's head and neck with all his strength, Morio rocked backwards pulling the weight of the man onto his crimped neck. Suddenly Morio was filled with fear. If he released the gendarme, there was no telling what he would do. So Morio held all the tighter as if he just wanted to stop time. The man's breathing passages were crumpling, and he was desperately gasping for air. He struggled to find any way possible to get Morio to release his hold on him.

4

Morio could feel the policeman's hands and fingers fumbling around his face clawing for something to grab and dig into. Morio kept shaking his head around to avoid his fingers. Suddenly he found the fingers of the policeman's right hand in his mouth, and he bit them as hard as he could. His teeth were sharp and his jaw powerful. He could feel and hear him crush the bones of the policeman's fingers and soon blood was flowing into his mouth. He tasted salt and iron as he swallowed the surge of blood to avoid choking on it.

Choking and gasping for whatever air he could get, the man struggled, pleaded for release, cursed his strangler hoarsely, and eventually could only eliminate low guttural sounds. It only took another minute or two and the policeman, having evacuated both his bowels and bladder, lay limp and journeying to whatever beyond might await him.

"Good heaven's you killed him!" Ono screamed at Morio. Ono had been too slow in getting back up to intervene and prevent the homicide. As they began to frenetically fuss about the policeman's body, Morio, his nerves causing his body to quake, pleaded, "I did not mean to. I was just afraid that if I let go, he would hurt me or us."

"It is a fate earned by this brutish Japanese vandal," Ono said collecting his thoughts about what to do next. "There is nothing we can do about it now except to try to make sure nobody ever finds out about this. I only hope that this will not bring down hellfire on us for despoiling Amamikyu's shrine." Ono quickly approached the shrine and placed the section of the cow's heart on an altar. He solemnly prayed for forgiveness for what had just transpired and asked that Morio be spared any divine retribution. Looking fervently and reverently downwards at the foot of the shrine, Ono muttered under his breath:

"Beitan shidai tongzhi Zhe
Baohu women cong
Womende weilai" He repeated it three times.

With his voice hinting of a touch of terror, Morio implored his father, "What was that you just said. Wasn't that Chinese?"

"Yes son," Ono looked up first at him and then at heaven.

"It is a saying, prayer actually, for the Lord of Time to preserve us from our future. I learned it years ago from one of the Chinese merchants who used to come here."

"Why would you say that within earshot of Amamikyu?"

"Son, in times of crisis and extreme peril, one should not be too finicky as to who or what might be invoked for aid."

Returning to the immediate situation, Morio exclaimed "What are we going to do? What are we going to do?"

"Get ahold of yourself, son. Look around, is anyone else here right now?"

"I don't think so. I don't think anyone saw what happened."

"Good, then," Ono said. "We better get rid of the body before anyone else comes to the shrine."

"But where? How?"

"We can drag him down the hill a little bit and stuff him in one of the caves there." Ono was directing Morio to grab the policeman's feet while he clasped his arms and lifted the torso. Struggling a bit, descending the hill in a rocking motion, they awkwardly maneuvered the body.

When they got to one of the several caves, with some difficulty they dragged the body into the cave. "We must stuff him as far back in the cave as possible," Ono instructed. "Even if it is ever discovered nobody will be able to know how it got here or how he died. Now go back and fill the jug with the water from the well and be quick about it!"

As they walked a little, something began to turn over and over in Morio's mind. "Father, what did you mean back there 'preserve us from our future'?

"The future is a very complex place, son. Youngsters like yourself look forward into it with hopeful anticipation of the great things that you can experience and achieve."

"Then why might we fear it?"

"In reality the future is like a dark cave. It might hold treasures and achievements for us but it can also hold snares, traps and grief. A life-ending misfortune just occurred there in front of

6

Amamikyu. Who knows what sort of scale balancing may have been set in motion?" Morio became quiet and slipped into pondering what his father just said.

With a full jug, they returned to the compound and tried to act as if nothing had happened. Ono strictly insisted that Morio could not tell anyone about the incident, not even his best friend Rin. The feast was conducted and gradually Morio rebounded to his more normal self. Still, he worried about what had happened and what might yet happen.

A few days before, a strange man had been circulating in the environs and even came to the compound trying to recruit agricultural workers for contract labor in a place far distant. He bragged about all the benefits of going to a place called Hawaii to work in the sugar cane fields. Claiming that Hawaii was a tropical island not unlike Okinawa, the man appealed to anyone who would listen bragging about the good money one could make there. Anyone brave enough to accept the adventurous challenge could send back enough money for their families to live comfortably and perhaps even buy some land to set themselves up for generations to come.

Morio and Rin had listened to the man but were rather uninterested. Ono and some of the elders lent an ear to the man's presentation with a little more mature interest borne of a foreboding over the continued deterioration of the family's fortunes since the Japanese had begun to absorb Okinawa into its empire back in 1872. The fellow said he would remain in the capital city Naha, not too far away from the compound, for a few more days to give a chance for volunteers to make up their minds and accept his offer.

The next day after the festival, Ono collected Morio, and they went for a walk.

"I think you have to go," Ono said with a sad look on his face. "Given the situation, it might be best for you to be away from here for a while."

"But, father, I..." Morio started to mount his protestations.

7

"If it is true that you can make money and send it back, then that would be good for the family as well."

"This is my home," Morio continued to argue.

"Right, and you have responsibilities to this home – a responsibility to keep dishonor from its gates and to help sustain the bodies and souls here."

Without any choler in his voice, Ono turned back all of Morio's pleas against any exile. It was decided and as head of the family, it was Ono's task to quickly convince the rest of the family of Morio's departure and outfitting him to go. It would be hard on everyone, but it seemed the best course of action.

For the rest of the day, Ono and Morio swung into action to get him ready to join the recruiter Toyama in Naha. They sent word to Toyama that Morio would join him the following day. Morio preferred to say goodbye to his mother and all the other members of the community at the compound. Only Ono and Rin went with him to Naha and met Toyama and the thirty-nine other recruits he had gathered. Ono, Morio, and Rin were silently brave as the whole contingent went to the docks. As the troop boarded the *SS Satsuma-maru* for passage to Osaka, Morio was somber reflecting on the twist of fortune forcing his farewell from his father, friend, and home. He quietly prayed:

"Beitan shidai tongzhi Zhe
Baohu women cong
Womende weilai

2

It was Saturday morning and the June gloom common to southern California was beginning to burn off promising another warm, bright, and sunny day. Twelve-year-old Eiji Takara lived in cramped quarters in Santa Monica with a gaggle of people. There was his father, Morio, mother Kiku, and Aimi, his older sister. Then there was his "uncle's" family. He really was not his uncle but a close friend of his father's from the plantation days in Hawaii. Yo Jahana and his father had been recruited as agricultural workers for the Hawaiian sugar plantations to escape their difficult and limited life prospects in Okinawa decades ago. Yo was from Naha, the city not far distant from where Morio was born and raised. They met as they were herded onto the *SS Satsuma-maru* and started to be friends. Even before their ship cleared sight of Naha harbor, Morio had already begun to miss his friend Kineshiro and, as they both crossed the ocean into a great unknown, they began to look to each other for support. They bonded much more deeply as they endured the harsh conditions for sugar workers in Hawaii. Having escaped the painful plantations and gotten to California, neither of them talked much about their experiences in Hawaii. Morio once mentioned that when he was sick, Yo had conspired with the plantation cooks to smuggle him some extra soup to help nurse him back to health. Not too long after that, Morio had met and married his wife Kiku and Yo had been his best man and a stand-in for his Okinawan family at the ceremony. During the bitter struggle and strike by Japanese workers in 1909, they protected each other as best they could from the thugs hired by the plantation owners to coerce and even beat the workers back into the fields. When they were evicted from their shabby shanties and left homeless, they gathered their wives and painfully trekked from their plantation into Honolulu. It was then that they decided to strike out for the mainland.

Landing in California, they remained friends and partners. To generate income as soon as possible, they joined other Japanese working the fields in and around Oxnard, California. Despite the more common disdain Japanese had for Okinawans back in Japan, they were not too badly received by other Japanese immigrants in California. It seemed that in the face of Anglo hostilities, Japanese residents felt that a little Japaneseness was better than none. And being on the outs of the Anglo power and privilege system, the Japanese workers could and did find some common causes with other suppressed people, like the Mexicans. Less than a decade prior, in 1903, the Japanese workers in the Oxnard fields banded with Mexican workers in perhaps the first multi-racial labor union and won some minor concessions in a fierce struggle against the growers there. But eventually, wearied by such struggles, they were able to pool their resources and set up a vegetable and fruit stand in Santa Monica, living together as a "family" to save money and provide mutual support. Eiji's "uncle" and "aunt" had a son, Saburo Jahana, just nine months younger than Eiji. The two of them were the very best of friends and did nearly everything together, as they were likely to do that Saturday.

As the day was beginning to unfold, Eiji's sister Aimi was getting ready for her Girl Scout meeting. She was fixing and fussing with her uniform to make sure that she had everything just right. She loved the uniform and everything about the Girl Scouts. She used to say that when she was wearing that uniform, she felt protected – protected against doubts about who and what she might be. Like her troopmates, she wanted so much to fit into the American world and society around them and dispel the questions and queries born of the impolite and oftentimes ignorant. "Where are you from?" would start the usual interrogation. "Right here, born in Santa Monica," she would answer. "No, I mean, where are you REALLY from?" The interlocutor surveying her face would try to guess if she were Chinese, Japanese, possibly Korean, or what. But in her shield uniform, she and her friends could engage in

10

quintessentially American activities and usually generate a reassuring smile or two from witnesses. The curious or suspicious sensed that the "foreign" looking girls were "assimilating" and becoming Americans and it made them feel better about the qualities and attributes of Americanness.

Meanwhile, Eiji and "cousin" Saburo were settling into their common bickering over who was going to read which comic book and who "owned" which illustrated tome of adventures and excitement. As fans of *The Detective Story Hour* on the radio which they tried to never miss, they had been elated when the *Shadow Magazine* began to appear first once a month then twice a month. Knowing the evil that lurked in the hearts of men, the Shadow fought crime and aurally tried to teach, via the radio waves, America's youth the evils of the bitter fruit the weeds of crime produce. The comics delivered similar messages and intrigues as the Shadow dealt with the "Silent Seven" or the "Black Master". The two of them had dedicated ten cents of their combined resources to purchasing the little detective/mystery novels and they had a collection of a dozen or so of them. Their good-natured negotiations over who got which book to read and re-read were part of the general cacophony of their household as everyone else went about their business preparing for the day. Their mothers shushed them at regular intervals and reminded them of the chores that had to do.

Their dive into the shadowy world of detective discoveries was discontinued when they broke to take up their assigned household tasks. As they went about sweeping and cleaning, they called out to each other plans for what they might do after they were finished. They decided they would get dressed up in their cowboy outfits and try to get permission to go to the movies. As much as they feasted on *The Shadow* comics, they probably loved going to the movies even more. Westerns were their favorite as they were thrilled at the episodes of good guys vanquishing savages, protecting the innocent, and preserving justice in the tumultuous world of the wild west. They did not get to go to the movies very often so the catalog of films that they had seen was thin. "Cimarron" and "Fighting Caravans", with Gary Cooper, were two of their favorites. They had heard of a new movie coming out, "Texas Pioneers", starring Bill Cody and they wanted to get to see it if they could. Like his sister, Eiji liked wearing his "uniform" of sorts – a cowboy hat and a plaid shirt. He wished that he could have one of the hats and perhaps one of the blue shirts that the cavalry heroes wore in the movies. That uniform for sure would signify his righteousness and strike fear in the hearts of desperadoes and the Cheyenne or Sioux alike. Doing his imaginary part in establishing and maintaining peace for the benefit of humble settlers taming the west made him feel Americanly important.

One of the other derivatives of their love of movies was that Eiji began to develop a unique "skill". He had a very good ear for voices, accents, and intonation. Over time he got very good at impersonating movie actors and accurately imitating their speech. This added to their mutual enjoyment of the movies because often, after seeing a movie, Eiji would act out add-on or continuation scenes providing authentically sounding dialogue of the major characters they had just seen. This meant that creatively Eiji and Saburo could continue to escape into the worlds of their heroes until the next movie they were allowed to see.

But just then Morio came into the house and called Eiji over to him. "Get yourself cleaned up a bit, your uncle and I are taking you on a little trip." Eiji heard his father but did not know what he was talking about. "What?" he asked. "Don't ask questions, just get ready," came his father's clipped order. "But ..but Saburo and I were ..."

"Just do as I say," His father said leaving no doubt that Eiji had better comply. "This involves your future."

So, Eiji looked disappointedly at Saburo who had heard the exchange and understood Eiji's predicament. They both knew that something else was looming in less than two weeks that would separate the two of them for who knew how long. With shoulder shrugs, they both looked at each other as Eiji followed his father out of the house and towards their pickup truck with Uncle Yo.

Eiji Takara just stood there for a minute slowly surveying what his father and uncle had excitedly brought him to see. The land was flat and dusty and stretched for quite a distance towards the ocean. Off in the distance to his left, he could see the shadowy outlines of a couple of islands that lay not far distant offshore. Looking straight ahead there was the hint of a town or little city with a somewhat strange name – Oxnard. He did not then know but further west from there was the settlement "Hollywood-by-the-Sea" so named because the 1926 blockbuster, "The Sheik" starring Rudolph Valentino, was filmed in the dunes of what was then known as Oxnard Beech. Behind him were the jagged teeth of coastal mountains and hills almost as a thin wall between where they were and Los Angeles to the east. The three of them had ridden in his father's pride and joy, a 1927 Ford Model T truck, along the sometimes breathtakingly scenic Roosevelt Highway, past the terminus of the mountains and onto the plain before them. Eiji too could imagine the area being the setting of any number of cowboy and Indian films that he and Saburo liked so much, and he began imagining charging and retreating across the land in his uniform battling the evil that lurked in men's hearts and the savagery of the frontier.

Eiji watched with great interest as his father and uncle walked across a rectangle of land marked by four white stakes driven into its corners. They were gesticulating excitedly, which was a bit out of the norm for his usually taciturn father. From what Eiji could grasp they were enthusiastically planning out their future in both their native Okinawan and quick, sharp Japanese, pointing both towards Oxnard and then back towards Los Angeles. He could not remember when, if ever, he had seen his father as happy and buoyant. Yo was usually the more demonstrative person in the family. But today his father seemed to be riding the crest of some wave of opportunistic possibilities.

After a few minutes, another pickup truck came bouncing across the dirt road and fields towards them. This one was a bit more beat up and deformed by nicks and dents than Eiji's father's truck. And when it came to a stop, an older Japanese man got out clad in carefully maintained but well-worn work clothes. The patches on his clothes were almost like embroidery, meticulously and artfully done by some precise hand and eye. Eiji did not recognize the man but from the deferentially formal and polite *sonkeigo* greetings that his father and uncle extended to the man, it seemed that his father at least knew him from somewhere. Eiji knew the vocabularies of polite, respectful, and humble Japanese language pretty well since his family was from Okinawan origins, they were always a notch below "real" Japanese on the social and class ladders. Izzy Otani was the son of Toraichi Otani, a struggling Japanese immigrant from Hiroshima who had come to the United States in 1898 and landed in Oxnard, California in 1902, just a year before the city was incorporated and the notorious strike of 1903.

Toraichi was an energetic entrepreneur if there ever was one and though he lost most of his money from various activities in Oxnard in the stock market crash of 1929 – he stoically reorganized his family and his affairs to try to rebound. Born in Oxnard, Izzy grew up fitting himself into the American world as best as he could. Graduating from high school in 1929, having been a notable athlete in at least four sports and active in other school clubs, he enrolled in UCLA in 1930 hoping to eventually get a law degree. To help pay his school expenses, Izzy worked at a fruit stand in Santa Monica where Eiji's father also worked.

As the adult men talked, Eiji's mind began to wander. He started drawing Japanese characters in the dust near him with his feet and wondered why they were there. Catching only snippets of the conversation, it had something to do with the land they were inspecting. Apparently, they were going to buy it. At that, Eiji's father called him over and introduced him to Izzy.

"Eiji, meet your new partner, Otani-san."

Eiji shot a quizzical glance upwards at his father while he bowed properly to Otani-san.

"Yes, Musuko, you and Otani-san are going to be the owners of these twenty acres of land here," Eiji's father said stomping the ground with his feet. Uncle Yo closed in with the three of them and smiling from ear to ear approvingly patted Eiji on the back.

But I am only twelve years old, Eiji thought. Also, he knew that upon the insistence of his father, he was scheduled to return to Okinawa in eleven days – so how could he own land or do anything with it? More importantly, why would he own land?

Tucked into the fabric of California's racist response to Asian immigration, first by Chinese and then by Japanese plantation workers leaving Hawaii and flowing into California in the early 1900s, was the Alien Land Registration Act of 1913. That piece of discriminatory legislation sought to undercut the successes the Japanese agricultural workers had been achieving after their arrival by prohibiting "aliens ineligible for citizenship" from purchasing and owning land. Stemming from the Nationality Act of 1790, the opportunity to become a naturalized citizen of the United States had consistently been reserved for "white persons" and though the Naturalization act of 1870 had extended that right to "aliens of African nativity and to persons of African descent" state and federal courts had consistently ruled Asians as ineligible. Hence, the first generation of Japanese immigrants, the Issei, were barred from the security of owning the land they sowed and brought to fruition. But Izzy and Eiji were born in the United States and therefore citizens by birth and the prohibitions of the laws did not apply to them.

All of this was explained to Eiji on the ride back to Santa Monica. The Otani and Takara families were going to pool their resources and buy a piece of land at a good price as a result of the distress of the owners due to the Depression. Then Eiji's father and Uncle Yo, and maybe some of Izzy's brothers, would work the land and send the produce to the stand their mother operated in Santa Monica and a proposed grocery store of Izzy's in Oxnard. It would all be a variant of the hard work and the struggles both families had been enduring for years, only this time by owning the land there would be a degree of legal security and safety undergirding their sweat and toil.

"But you are sending me back to Okinawa, next week?" Eiji interjected.

"Yes, we are, that is so you can be fully immersed in Okinawan and Japanese culture and society. We hope a few years there will reestablish some family ties, reinforce your understanding and respect for who you are, and become a better Japanese person. We are but a few Okinawans in a sea of Japanese here in America. The more effectively we can meld into the Japanese American community the better for our future. "

"But..but"

"And when you return you will be able to comfortably live and succeed in all worlds –America, Japanese America, and Japanese. "

The intent and design of the grand plan were opaque to Eiji. Leaving his natal family and venturing so far away to the company of unfamiliar and distant relatives in a strange place did not appeal to him. He had no connate desire to be a "better Japanese". He was perfectly happy navigating the challenges of being an American of Japanese descent. Not unaware of some of the bolts and barbs thrust at Japanese from inhospitable Americans, he was deft at dodging them and finding the sanguine spaces of youthfulness. He worried that being a "better Japanese" might lessen his Americanness. But he had no choice, he had to obey his father and embark on the plan. At about the same age, his father had departed Okinawa to start his new life on this side of the Pacific Ocean. He tried to be confident that he could juggle and balance everything so that upon his return he would most certainly be a better version of himself. As for being American, well, at least now he owned a piece of America and that might be the anchor he needed to stabilize his ship as he sailed to his uncertain fate.

3

The weather had warmed up considerably as the lightly clad Eiji and a family associate bid goodbye to the assembled families and friends at Long Beach harbor that first week in July. America was preparing for its annual Fourth of July celebrations while also staging a presidential election. The nominee of the Democratic Party, Franklin Delano Roosevelt, was battering the incumbent Republican President Herbert Hoover who was being blamed for the national agonies of the Great Depression. But Eiji was nervously focused on what lay across the sea. The pair had booked passage back to Japan on a cargo ship bound for Yokohama. The elder male was returning to Japan to attend to some family business, and, he had agreed to help shepherd Eiji safely as far as Japan proper. Eiji's mother was greatly relieved that her young son would not cross the Pacific alone and friendless. Morio cast his gaze beyond the harbor to the open sea and received a cascading cache of memories of his departure from Okinawa those many years ago.

It took eleven days to cross the ocean and Eiji was filled with doubts, fears, and gnawing uncertainties. The plan was that once they got to Yokohama, the friend would help Eiji arrange for the second leg of the trip – passage to Naha, Okinawa. He sent a telegram to Okinawa about Eiji's arrival in Japan and that he would be on the Wednesday ferry which should make Naha harbor some thirty to forty hours later. That should give Eiji's family enough time to arrange a welcome committee to gather him and get him to his new home.

Since the formal annexation of Okinawa into the Japanese political sphere sixty years prior to Eiji's arrival, metropolitan Japan relentlessly displaced the former Okinawan elite. At the behest of the Emperor of Japan, the King of Okinawa was retired and coopted into a comfortable sinecure in Kyoto. Eiji's distant relatives were part of a trading/mercantile class that had managed trade between Okinawa and China. For a century or more, his paternal family had worked hard, prospered, and acquired extensive properties and trade businesses. His father's meager efforts in Santa Monica were a variation of a long-standing family interest and tradition in business. But the family's position and wealth were eroded seriously when those trading patterns were liquidated after the Japanese thrashing of China in the Sino-Japanese War of 1895. Beginning shortly thereafter the Imperial Japanese government commenced dogged efforts to amalgamate the islands more fully into the larger definition of Japan. Surrendering to the obvious and inevitable, his family members were founding members of an accommodationist organization, the Kai-ka in 1903.

sought to moderate the arrogant aggressiveness of the burgeoning cadre of Japanese administrators and preserve some Okinawan voice in civic affairs. In 1903, the land reform project of the central government was complete, further displacing Okinawan grandees and saddling what was left of that class with draining taxes. Not too long after that as a laboratory for managed popular participation in government, the Okinawan Prefectural Assembly was convened which subsequently led to the sending of representatives to the Imperial Diet. The political climates of Japan and Okinawa were mercurial and sometimes violently temperamental between a bevy of factions on the mainland and the simmering tensions between the Okinawans and the Japanese on the island. Essentially Eiji was muddling into multiple minefields, some historic and others contemporary, that would require the utmost dexterity to navigate without disaster.

As arranged by his chaperone, Eiji was met at Naha harbor by a small contingent of his family members, none of whom he had ever met or seen before, who enthusiastically welcomed him "home" as if retrieving a lost sheep. His presence instantly re-established consanguinity connections through an agnate grandson. As the group made its way by streetcar and then pedicab to the family compound on the outskirts of the city, there was a continuous chatter in a pidgin fusion of Tokyo dialect Japanese and Okinawan hogen that Eiji had to race through all his linguistic experiences to keep up with. What he did not fully understand, he derived enough meaning from context to nod and answer questions about the "American" side of the family and his journey to their midst. Challenged though he was, his keen ear for languages, dialects, and accents kicked in and organized the words, verbs, and voices he was bombarded with into sensible intercourse.

As the delegation and the newcomer approached the gate of a walled compound of the Takara clan, Eiji noticed the large sign posted reading "Welcome to 'Some Place Else'". He wondered about it but refrained from asking as the residents of the compound all flowed from their hovels and their labors to greet the returnees from the city. More introductions were conducted with Eiji properly bowing and respectfully greeting an unanticipated collection of non-relatives. Everyone was commenting on their good fortune to have Eiji join them as both a returning family member but also the seventeenth person to take up residence in the compound. Seventeen was considered a propitious and especially lucky number and many of the group nodded approvingly about how Eiji might help improve the fortunes of the little community. Surveying the faces and trying to fix names to the constituents of the little colony, Eiji noticed that the ages of the little hamlet he was joining ranged from babies to his grandparents in their 80s. A man named Rin Kineshiro who seemed to have some authority introduced himself to Eiji. His father had spoken of Kineshiro many times and Eiji was glad to finally meet him. Noticing the boy's puzzled looks, Kineshiro san began to explain how it was that everyone was crammed together in the traditional Takara estate complex. Eiji noticed that his grandfather stood behind Kineshiro san as to verify and approve of what was being said. Being one of the most prominent families of the merchant aristocrats, the Takaras were allowed to keep their complex and a moderate amount of their land during the successive reorganization of the politics and economics of Okinawa since Japan's imperial expansion after 1895. The Kineshiro clan and the Takara clan had been closely aligned, partners, and friends for many, many years. When the Japanese began their process of "modernizing" Okinawa, the Kineshiro's had most of their land appropriated by the land reform process and were essentially evicted from their estate. When they asked the Japanese authorities, what could they do and where might they go, the uniform reply was: "Go somewhere else."

Motioning to a few other people, "The same thing happened to them," Eiji's grandfather added. "We had the space and the moral obligation to offer aid and hospitality to our compatriots and that is how the Ahanes, Miyagis, and Yamashiros came to join us as well. They were all told to "go live somewhere else,'" the grandfather said almost shamefully with a touch of pity in his voice.

"But we have banded together, and we will persevere," announced Kineshiro san. "We have organized ourselves, assigning leadership roles, responsibilities, and tasks to everyone," he optimistically said with a touch of pride. "I am in charge of all agricultural activities."

Kineshiro san began to give almost a report on the communal activities under his purview. "We grow a little sugar cane on fields just beyond that hill over there. Here you can see the vegetable gardens that the women tend to. You see goya growing there next to the shuibui, and daikon. The purple sweet potatoes and taro are over there to the right of the moui. Down over there we have nigana and a good amount of handama growing."

It was all a bit much for Eiji to take in all at once. Sensing that, his grandmother approached and gently began to lead him to a large table set with numerous dishes of various kinds as the welcome feast for him. Only then did Eiji realize that he was hungry and much appreciated the opportunity to attend to that. As everyone gathered around the table and began to enjoy the feast, pockets of little conversation broke out and Eiji did his best to answer the questions everyone had about his journey and most particularly about America. Not too long had passed when the light, free and easy air of the time was polluted by a very distinct odor coming from the direction of the gate. Everyone immediately knew who was approaching and a seriously guarded pall overcame them all.

Eiji looked in the direction of the gate and saw a man in uniform advancing on them. The Japanese police deputy always gave off fair warning of his approach by his fragrance. Fastidious about his appearance, Deputy Sato never went out into public without bathing thoroughly and the modern soap, manufactured on the Japanese mainland, exuded a distinctive fragrance. People could literally smell Deputy Sato from around corners before he arrived. Self-assuredly smiling broadly, the Deputy audaciously waltzed up to the table, picked up a pair of chopsticks, and began to sample the dishes without so much as a by-your-leave.

"Deputy Sato, how good of you to join us on this auspicious occasion. We are welcoming our cousin and friend Eiji Takara back home from his adventures in America."

"I know," Deputy Sato said curtly reaching for the best part of the salt grilled Gurukun fish and subsequently stuffing it in his mouth rolling his eyes with pleasure at the deliciousness of the morsel. Reaching then for a sample of goya chanpuru, he informed the gathering, "I came to inspect Eiji's papers and to officially welcome him on behalf of the Imperial government and Governor Jiro Ino. We expect and hope that he will be a positive addition to the welfare of the prefecture."

Kineshiro san quickly grabbed Eiji and pushed him toward Deputy Sato signaling to him to bow most reverently to the Deputy. "I am sure he will. We'll make sure he knows what is up here and how he can best serve everyone's needs," prodding Eiji to affirm the testament.

Eiji stumbled, almost forgetting his most formal and gracious greetings, "A, a, yes, I come to learn how to be a better Japanese servant and person."

Deputy Sato was pleased with Eiji's averment. Surrendering to his sweet tooth, Deputy Sato briskly and rather impolitely pushed past Kineshiro san and pounced on the platter of kippan treats. On his way he noticed Eiji's grandfather casting a disapproving glance at him. "What are you looking at old man?" the Deputy challenged.

"Poor is the person who does not know when he has had enough," Grandfather Ono said.

"I'll be the judge of when I've had enough," the Deputy growled. "Those look delicious, and I think I'll have two!"

"Wisdom is lost in a fat man's body," observed Ono.

Almost instinctively Deputy Sato raised his arm brandishing his cane and threateningly gestured towards Grandfather Ono. Equally instantly Kineshiro san and several other adult males moved to block and head off the Deputy. Eiji's grandmother quoted the proverb: "Happiness rarely keeps company with an empty stomach," and graciously invited the Deputy to help himself.

The Deputy returned to his arrogant officious self and snarled at Kineshiro san, "Remember, your taxes are due next week. You should consider paying them in full and not one mon less," was Sato's emphatic command. He then grabbed another kippan, wheeled, and strode out of the compound taking his smells of different kinds with him. Slowly the party reignited from the embers of their earlier joy. Eiji had his first lesson in the political science of being an Okinawan in the Japanese world. The average mainland Japanese citizen looked upon Okinawans as savages and uncouth near aboriginal barbarians.

For purposes of reputation and prestige, the Japanese government was doing what it could to "upgrade" the Okinawans in a world that had been carved up by European powers into colonial satrapies. Trying to measure up to the westerners who had imposed some of their unequal, discriminatory, and racist tenets on Japan, a massive and often frenetic series of reforms and transformations sought to remake Japan into a modern co-equal empire. The British, French, Germans, and Americans all had their versions of empires suggesting that imperialism itself was one of the hallmarks of having achieved advanced civilization. Absorbing and uplifting the Okinawans would prove that the Japanese were as good at shouldering their civilizing responsibilities on larger stages as those who were taking up the "white man's burden" or the French "mission civilisatrice". Okinawa was a laboratory for Japanese policies of creating loyal and faithful subjects dedicated to the advancement of a greater imperial Japan. It was also a training and proving ground for imperial officials for them to master the art of governance of dissimilar and sometimes resistant populations.

After his first night's sleep in a hammock hung in what had previously been a tool shed in the former days of the estate, Eiji awakened to the hustle and bustle of the compound and the smell of miso soup simmering on the stove in the courtyard. He stumbled out to the courtyard and was shown where he could wash his face before breakfast. In addition to the miso soup, he had a kind of bread made from purple potatoes and turmeric and was urged to eat some nigana, a vegetable said to help maintain the health of one's stomach. The introductory and instructional conversations from his arrival began again and continued. It was obvious that everyone in the compound had their duties and assigned tasks and when he asked what his would be, his grandmother laughingly replied: "To go to school, of course." It seemed agreed to by all, his American family and his Okinawan family, that his sole duty and purpose was to burnish the family's reputation by distinguishing himself as a scholar and properly educated "Japanese" person. On one level that was acceptable to him as he loved to learn and had aspirations of getting a good education and returning to America better able to contribute to the family's fortunes. But on another level, while he was in Okinawa, he wanted to do something to aid the struggles of the clan and the compound. Quietly, to himself, he resolved to be on the lookout for opportunities to do what he could for the betterment of those around him.

After breakfast, his grandfather called for him to join him in a walk. They set out together, his grandfather leading the way, and they began to ascend the hills behind their compound. Eiji followed his grandfather, carrying a gourd bottle to collect water, through the slightly overgrown pathway accentuated by spindly Diego trees lifting the red fingers of their flowers to the heavens contrasted beautifully by the green of the pine trees on both sides of the path. He was amazed at the strength and vigor the old man still had. Well into his eighties, he was still nimbly stepping on the stones to avoid getting his feet wet in the little pools of water left from the heavy morning dew, occasionally casting experienced glances backward at the novitiate Eiji doing his best to keep up. They came to a little clearing that hosted a sizeable nearly flat boulder and the grandfather slowly lowered himself on it to pause for a smoke. Pulling a pouch of purple tobacco from his garment and a long pipe, he packed it and motioned to Eiji to light it.

"Sit and rest a bit, we'll be at this for most of the day," Grandfather Ono softly said.

"Where are we going?"

"The well at Seifa Utaki. That's what the vessel you are carrying is for. We'll fill it and take it back to the compound."

"But we have a well back in the compound, I saw people getting water from it this morning," Eiji wondered.

"Ah, but that is not the special water at Seifa Utaki."

Eiji asked the obvious question with his furrowed eyebrows.

"Seifa Utaki is a sacred place. It is where the goddess Amamikyu came down to earth and gave birth to we Okinawans. It is our most sacred place, though the Japanese have somewhat polluted it by making it a Shinto shrine."

There it was again, the Japanese wanting to avoid unnecessarily alienating the Okinawans and demonstrating their magnanimous fusion of Okinawan traditions into Japanese spirituality, they had incorporated into the world of Shintoism. So Japanese and Okinawans could go there to replenish their spirituality for similar but different reasons. But in reality, the Japanese "graciousness" was taken as an unwanted intrusion into the core of Okinawan civilization.

"The water there has special healing powers," Grandfather Ono said as he stood up, still toking on his pipe, and began striding further along the jungle path.

"Yes, once your cousin, Isamu, was bitten by a sea krait while harvesting some seaweed one night. The irabu is exceptionally poisonous and he was almost certain to die," taking another puff on his pipe as he stood to continue their walk. "While he was paralyzed and sweating profusely, we poured as much of the sacred water down his throat as we could. In three days, he came back to us and recovered fully."

Eiji was relieved at the resolution of the story but was almost humorously shocked by Grandfather Ono's final comment.

"Since he held on to the snake as he initially struggled, we had a celebratory feast at his recovery. They are really delicious," Grandfather Ono smiled. "Now that you are here, we need to keep some extra elixir around. You are not likely to encounter an Irabu but there are plenty of Habu snakes in the jungle and their bites can be serious and life-threatening as well."

The rest of their journey to the shrine and the gathering of the water was largely quiet but interspersed with Grandfather Ono's observations about the spirits and demons that were reputed to frequent the area. At one point he pointed out a nest of caves to the right of their pathway but warned Eiji not to venture into them. It was all fascinating to Eiji as he drank in the commentary and what it revealed about traditional Okinawan culture. Personally, he did not believe in spirits or demons but that did not matter. In America, the family had occasionally flirted with Methodism by going to services at the Los Angeles Holiness Church and listening to the sermons of pastor Sadaichi Kuzuhara. The church had been founded in 1921 by six Issei Japanese and was focused specifically to serve the needs of the Japanese population of Los Angeles. His parents were not particularly enthusiastic about the theology and doctrine but the whole family did enjoy the occasional immersion in the larger Japanese and Japanese American community. Their association with the congregation did sometimes have benefits for their business as well when church members patronized their produce stand.

4

Eiji's main responsibility was to go to and do well in school enhancing the reputation and the possible future fates of the family in the process. He and Kineshiro san went slightly more than two miles into Shashiki, the capital of the First Sho dynasty of the Ryukyu Kingdom in the late 14th century, the nearest settlement with a government-established school. They completed all the forms and paperwork necessary to get him enrolled in the school there. Eiji would start out in the upper level of the primary education there in Shashiki. Judging by how well he did and fit in, he might be able to and better off if he transferred to one of the middle schools in Naha about ten miles from "Some Place Else".

The educational system of Japan and eventually Okinawa had been undergoing transformations and reforms since the Japanese reforms of the Meiji Restoration of the 1860s. In the 1890s in an attempt to grow an Okinawan contingent in the bureaucracy the middle school in Naha graduated a few students who entered government service and the normal school began to generate teachers to serve in the expanding educational network of the Ryukyu Islands. It was about then that a trickle of Okinawans volunteered for training as non-commissioned officers in the Japanese army, but the central government still did not trust Okinawans in general enough to enfold them into the Japanese conscription system for mainstream army service. Over the succeeding years, back-and-forth tensions between Okinawans resentful at the disrespectful and discriminatory treatment at the hands of multiple educational administrators and the provincial government wanting to ameliorate the tensions and more effectively assimilate Okinawans into Japan produced student strikes and government concessions. Eventually, around the turn of the century, the Japanese garrison at Shuri Castle was withdrawn and replaced by a native Okinawan garrison made up of conscripts through their acceptance in that system. Subsequentially a second and later a third middle school was established, including the admittance of women, and by the late 1920s Okinawan attendance in some level of schooling reached almost 99%.

Eiji and Kineshiro san returned to "Some Place Else". There was some discussion about how Eiji might get to and from his classes in Shashiki and possibly later in Naha. The first suggestion was that he could walk to and from Shashiki as he was young and strong. But some pointed out that he would have to leave early and get back late and the journey, short as it might be, might tire him out and impact his performance in the classroom. It was suggested that he might ride the family's horse which delighted Eiji to no end as he would have to learn to ride a horse in the process. As a wannabe cowboy in his American imagination and leisure activities

27

with Saburo, actually riding a real horse was almost the fulfillment of his dreams. Over the next couple of days, he practiced riding the horse with different members of the community.   The horse was old and mild so it was not difficult, and it is likely that the horse could get to Shashiki and back on its own with a little practice. Eiji even broke out his authentic cowboy hat that he had brought from America to put himself in "uniform" and complete his fanciful flights into the world of justice and honor in the old west.

After further discussion about the practicality of Eiji riding the horse to school and leaving it there all day for his return trip, the community suggested that he use the aged, but still functional, Fuji bicycle. It was rusted and banged up a bit making it unattractive to potential thieves, but with a little lubrication, it would work just fine. Of course, Eiji already knew how to ride a bicycle so the only thing he needed to do was to map out a route back and forth from the school. This he did with another member of the compound, about the same age, one on the horse and Eiji on the bicycle. The two of them agreed that Eiji might ride the horseback from the school just for fun. The bicycle was much more practical if and when he went to school in Naha. He would have to board there during the week but on the weekends, he could ride home to refresh himself in the loving embrace of his family and "Some Place Else".

Eiji also got his first packet from his sister Aimi back in the United States. He was very excited as he had heard nothing about the family's affairs since he boarded the steamer to Japan. It was a packet because it included a small sampling of Eiji's favorite hard candy and a pair of socks. But it was the letter written in English, so Eiji would not forget his English, that excited him the most. Things seemed to be going well enough for the family. His father and uncle Yo had sown their first crops on "his" land near Oxnard and were optimistic about their prospects. The produce market in Santa Monica was doing its usual business. His mother continued to bake and sell her taiyaki cakes. Aimi went on at some length about her Girl Scout activities and even included a picture of her in her beloved uniform. She looked so happily American. Several paragraphs were dedicated to Saburo and his exploits. Everyone expressed how much they missed him and while reading the letter, Eiji felt the same.

While waiting for the school sessions to begin, Eiji did whatever he could around the compound to be helpful and demonstrate his gratitude for their hospitality. True he was a "family" member, but still, his presence did add a bit to the strain on the family's meager resources. He always listened carefully to what he was told and what was said. In the evenings, he would try to draw out some of his grandfather's memories and stories about the past, the family, and the world he had known over his years. His grandfather had a melodic voice which Eiji began to quietly alone imitate until he felt he got it down pretty accurately.

One night after the evening meal, he thought he would try out his impersonation on the diners. He stood and raised his arms in a gesture of greeting and hospitality. He began. "Thank you all for coming here today. You give me so much honor to share my repast. I am especially happy to have my young grandson from America here with us." Startled a bit, everyone looked up at Eiji at first confused as to who was actually speaking. When they realized it was Eiji, they looked to Grandfather Ono for his reaction. Grandfather Ono broke out laughing, saying: "It seems that I now have two voices. Thank you, other voice, for expressing the views I have been keeping to myself." At that everyone laughed and complemented Eiji on his skill and talent.

"Hey Eiji, can you do other voices," someone called out.

"Sure," Eiji replied. He then did a collection of American movie stars but quickly realized that the accuracy of his mimicry was lost on an audience who were not familiar with the characters.

"What about radio voices," someone else asked?

"I could try," Eiji volunteered.

The compound commonly gathered around their one radio in the evenings but this time with a keener interest in the programs. Eiji listened to some of the characters and news commentators intensely. After a couple of evenings, he began to get the hang of impersonating a few of the radio voices much to the glee of the compound members. They encouraged Eiji to say what they might have preferred to hear from the news commentators than what was actually said. In a way, it did augment the attention various compound members paid to current events and provided a unique source of humor for all.

5

As his academic career began, Eiji was clearly a major outsider in the little hut transformed into a schoolhouse in Shashiki. Neither was he a "pure" Okinawan or "pure" Japanese but a hybrid of those two blended with his Americanness. His classmates did not really know how to relate to him, and they made fun of him behind his back – mainly because his Okinawan language skills were at best rudimentary. In accordance with government policy, students were forbidden to speak Okinawan at school, even though their teacher was himself an Okinawan. If anyone forgot and lapsed into the native language, they were punished by being made to wear a placard around their neck designating them as an offender. The only way the forgetful or recalcitrant student could escape the onus of the placard was to catch someone else speaking Okinawan and therefore transfer it to the newest uncompliant scholar. It might have been like a game, but it had such negative reverberations to it all that soon the students were speaking almost exclusively in Japanese. Of course, this was not really a problem for Eiji because if he switched out of Japanese, he was more likely to slide into English. When he did that, he actually gained the respect of his peers and the teachers who themselves knew virtually no English or any western languages at all. Everyone at the school was required to spend three hours a day studying Japanese to further break down Okinawan culture and loyalties and replace their ways of communicating and thinking with Japanese. All the strict focus on language issues did indeed help Eiji make rapid progress in improving his Japanese and better understand some of the Japanese customs and ways.

It did not take long for Eiji and everyone else to realize that the foundations of his American education set him apart from his classmates in Shashiki. This was especially true in mathematics and science. He tried to be properly humble and respectfully reserved in those areas especially when his instructors themselves struggled with concepts and the lessons. Sometimes, though, the teacher responsible for the science lessons floundered a bit. Since he spoke some English, Eiji might prompt him a bit in English which had the effect of enhancing both of their reputations as they could communicate in code unintelligible to anyone else.

While Eiji bounced back and forth between Shishaki and "Some Place Else" the whole island labored to recover from a severe typhoon that destroyed over 7,000 buildings in 1931 just before Eiji arrived. Always last on the list of provinces that received the attention and support of the central government, the Okinawans did their best to rebuild after the storm while still harboring resentments about their second-class status in the greater Japan.

After just one term at Shishaki, Eiji successfully transferred to one of the newer middle schools in Naha hoping to later ascend the academic ladder to some advanced education in Naha or even mainland Japan. Arrangements were made and Eiji moved into a dormitory in Naha number 2 middle school, which was newer and more modern, than the "premier" Middle School #1. He was issued the required military uniform for all boys and introduced to fundamental military training, behaviors, and expectations. Japan was at the time engaged in expanding its empire by detaching several provinces of northeastern China from the Republic of China and creating the fictionally independent puppet state of Manchukuo out of the traditional Manchurian homeland. To draw attention away from its nefarious behavior in Manchuria, pugilistic provocations were organized in Shanghai in January 1932 which spawned the "First Shanghai Incident". Underestimating the

Chinese willingness and abilities to fight, overconfident Japanese commanders initially bungled their tussle with Chinese troops. That ignited an outburst of emotional sensationalism as the spell-bound Japanese public lapped up the national press's praise of three soldiers who, having run out of ammunition, strapped explosives to themselves and tried to breach Chinese defenses in an unsuccessful suicide bomb attack.

The largest newspapers in Japan sponsored a poetry contest for fitting commemorative verses honoring the three heroes. Over 200,000 poems flowed into the offices of the newspapers and many of them were published. Eiji read some of them and tried to sort out how he felt about it all given his essentially triple identities. Soon, plays about the "three human bullets" flooded Japanese theaters and stages complete with the song "Three Human Bullets" sometimes performed with chorus lines kicking up their heels. Six movies were made about the self-sacrifice of the three warriors.

The Japanese public's taste for such histrionics was further whetted by the Major Kuga Noboru incident. A few weeks after the 'three bullets" incident, in February Major Kuga Noboru and his 200-man command found themselves surrounded by Chinese troops. The unit was mauled and the Major himself was badly wounded and taken prisoner. He was later returned to the Japanese in a prisoner exchange in March 1931. Feeling he had disgraced himself by not fighting to the last drop of his blood, he returned to the spot of his capture and committed suicide. Again, the literary and film world lionized Major Kuga labeling him as the perfect soldier and the embodiment of the ways of the warrior. Using his sacrifice as militaristic propaganda, five movies were made about him in 1932, the first released March 10, 1932.

As a lover of movies, Eiji did not hesitate to strain himself to see the silver screen hero-worship of the brave soldiers fighting for the cause of greater Japan. The films were stirring and exciting enough but to Eiji, at least, the cause the men were fighting for was less clear. He did not fully understand why the heroism of Chinese soldiers in fiercely defending their homeland was so abhorrent to Japan. Transitioning to his new surroundings at the middle school in Naha he joined the daily ritual of assembling in the courtyard in uniform to hear the rudimentary public announce system play the Japanese national anthem while the flag was raised. From the outset, he and all the students were fed a constant stream of patriotic promulgation asserting that Japan was the country of God, the best in the world. Other peoples in the world were inferior; the Chinese were called dirty chinks, the Russians pigs, and westerners hairy barbarians. That was difficult for Eiji to swallow as he knew from his own experiences that, though not perfect, the United States had its attractive sides to it. His experience with the Chinese in America had been reasonable and not noxious. As for Russians, he had no idea as to what they were really like.

On September 15, 1932, Japan and Manchukuo signed the Japan-Manchukuo Protocol that granted Japan the right to sustain its military forces in Manchukuo more or less formalizing and solidifying the unequal dominant and subordinate status of the two geographical and political entities. The world condemned the Japanese brazenness and both Manchurian and Chinese military units and Japanese soldiers clashed intermittently. Both on the continent and in the home islands, militarism was operating like yeast gobbling up the sugar in flour and expelling noxious carbon dioxide leavening both external and internal political dough. One could faintly detect the odor of gun grease in the atmosphere.

Again, Eiji was a curiosity in his school. He was some sort of platypus, part Japanese, part Okinawan, and part American. It was the American side of him that attracted some interest among his classmates. He was repeatedly questioned about what America was and what it was like to live there. Sometimes he even played up his Americanness by walking around campus after classes wearing his cherished cowboy hat.

Some of his classmates had seen a couple of American westerns and they asked him. "Do they really have cowboys in America?"

"Sure, but not so many anymore," Eiji would respond.

"Why?"

"Cowboys were mostly part of the old wild west in America. Now the western part of the country is pretty settled and tame."

"Is that where you are from?"

"Yes, I was born and live in California, the westernmost of the American states," Eiji would answer. "I could go down to the beach and see the Pacific Ocean from my house. If I looked out to the water, I could imagine Japan was just on the other side, far, far away."

"Is that hat part of the cowboy's uniform?" asked one classmate.

"I guess you could say that. There are a couple of different types of cowboy hats. I like this one best because it is the type worn by the actor John Wayne."

A stumped look came over the face of his friend who obviously did not know who John Wayne was.

"Did the cowboys fight Indians?" he asked, returning to the topic.

"Occasionally. But most of that was done by the American soldiers. They rode horses and were called the cavalry," Eiji said as he took off his hat and began to admire it a bit himself. "Sometimes, cavalrymen wore hats almost like this as part of their uniform."

The discussion then turned to the similarities and dissimilarities between American cowboys, the cavalry and Japanese samurai. They both were mounted warriors and fought bandits and indigenous populations deemed to be uncivilized. Americans fought Indians. On the northern island of Hokkaido, the samurai fought the Ainu and almost wiped them out. The same fate nearly happened to the Native Americans. Both the cowboys (at least the good ones) and the samurai symbolized courage, righteousness, and purity of heart and morals. Many tales were woven about them as illustrative examples of certain noble character traits.

For two years Eiji studied in Naha doing what he could to distinguish himself. When he would ride the rickety old bicycle back to "Some Place Else" he would wear his precious cowboy hat and pretend he was a cavalry scout sent out on some important and dangerous mission. In the company of his family, he would be questioned about the school and how he was doing. He did not want to brag so he fended off such questions with vague answers. Truth was, he was doing very well. He had attracted the notice of the senior teacher and principal of the school who thought Eiji had the potential to do well in a more challenging setting.

The governor of Okinawa prefecture then was Jiro Ino. Ambitious and anxious to involve Okinawa and his leadership more directly in the national affairs of Japan and the fortunes of the expanding Japanese Empire, the governor looked for any way possible way to call attention to what Okinawa might have to offer to the glory of Japan. Tokyo University of Commerce, a private institution of higher education established in 1920 and successfully eluding absorption into Tokyo University, had grown into Japan's premier institution of commercial education in the country. In 1923 the Kanto Earthquake destroyed all its buildings, save the library. Slowly it began to rebound and by 1930 was able to move to Kunitachi, fifteen miles west of central Tokyo. The new campus built there was quite impressive and sought to affirm its elevated status in the Japanese educational milieu. To celebrate its successes and to try to broaden its reputation throughout greater Japan, it began to offer a limited number of scholarships to students from distant prefectures to generate a truly national alumni of some of the brightest young minds in the nation and empire. Nominees for the scholarships had to pass a qualifying exam first. If they did, they could enroll in a program appropriate for their age and interest. One option was a regular degree-granting curriculum. The governor figured that if he could nominate someone and the Okinawan candidate could receive the scholarship, it might make his leadership and his efforts to improve the educational system of the prefecture glow a bit in the eyes of his superiors. He asked the principals of middle schools #1 and #2 if they had a student who might fit the bill.

The faculty at Eiji's middle school gathered in the teacher's conference room and heard the principal explain what the governor

35

was looking for and if they might suggest someone. There was a short murmur among the teachers and without much hesitation, Eiji was the nearly unanimous consensus of the faculty. Eiji was popular among the faculty for many reasons, not the least of which was constant willingness to help out in the classroom. Several of them offered to do some intense tutoring to help him prepare for the qualifying exam. Time would be short, but the assumption was that if Eiji would be willing to buckle down and cram for the exam he could surely do well.

When Eiji was presented with the honor and the possibility, he was not entirely sure how to respond.

"I would have to leave here and go to Tokyo?"

"Of course," said his favorite teacher who had been delegated to broach the issue with Eiji and convince him of the virtues of the special opportunity.

"And I would be studying business?"

"That's right and get a university degree from perhaps the finest business school in all of Japan."

"I am not sure what business studies would be like. I had not considered what I might do after I graduated from here. I am not even sure how much longer before I return to the United States. I will have to ask my father what he thinks."

"Of course, that is logical, and I understand. But I am sure he would approve of this good fortune," the teacher said reassuringly. "We could telegraph him today if you like and maybe you'll get a quick response. After all, he sent you here to get a good education and to enrich your Japanese heritage. Though you have become familiar with your family here in Okinawa, what better place to become deeply immersed in Japanese culture and society than in Tokyo?"

"What if I do not pass the exam or get selected?" Eiji pondered not sure of his abilities.

"Well, if that happens you can continue your education here, and then once you graduate, we can find a good path forward for you. Or you could return to the United States with some greater knowledge of both Okinawan and Japanese civilizations," the teacher said gently patting Eiji on the shoulder to reassure him.

Eiji thought about it for a few minutes and saw no harm in at least volunteering to try to earn the scholarship. Whatever would happen would happen, right? Maybe some business knowledge would come in handy back in America and he could help manage the family business. He remembered that technically, the farm near Oxnard was "his" farm.

A couple of days later his favorite teacher approached him and gave him his father's return telegram. Eiji read it as happy to just get some words from his father if for no other reason. In a few brief words, his father enthusiastically encouraged him and praised him for positioning himself for the great honor. Things could not have worked out better. Go and do your best, his father urged him and assured him that there would be great celebrations upon his return.

But Eiji also ached a bit from missing his family and life at his real home. "Some Place Else," and Okinawa were still "foreign" to him in so many ways. Perhaps that is what fueled his academic success as he distracted himself from what he missed and the pangs of loneliness by studying hard. Still, relocating to Tokyo could be exciting enough to help him endure his transpacific time.

It was settled then. Eiji would throw his cowboy hat into the ring and compete for the scholarship. The nomination was made and accepted. A packet of materials arrived at the governor's office from Tokyo with all the forms and explanations of what was to be done. The governor wanted to personally meet Eiji and take his measure while delivering the application materials to his school principal. A meeting was arranged.

With discernable zeal, governor Ino praised himself first for his wise and enlightened leadership of the prefecture which established the climate in which Eiji, and all students could grow and prosper. He and the larger Japanese administrative architecture of the burgeoning empire were engaged in the transformation of Asia and that bright young men like Eiji would be recruits in the beaming of the rays of the Japanese rising sun flowing across Japan and outward to the rest of the world. Liberating Manchuria from China and assisting in the building of an independent Manchurian home nation – Manchukuo -- began in 1931. The Tanggu Truce which had been concluded between Japan and the Nationalist Chinese in May 1933 formally ended what had been, to the Japanese, unfairly characterized internationally as the Japanese invasion of Manchuria. To them, pulling Manchuria out of the mud of the unstable, corrupt, backward, and incompetent government of Nationalist China under Chiang Kai-shek and his coterie of barely civilized warlords was a noble mission for Japan to undertake. Perhaps, upon completion of his studies, Eiji could help develop the business and commercial ties between Manchukuo and Japan contributing to the greater peaceful prosperity and security of both nations and the well-being of both nations.

Eiji was not so interested in the political pontifications of governor Ino as he was the unique patterns and cadence of his speech. His knowledge of the situation on the continent and concerning Manchukuo was confined to the carefully manicured information shared out by the Ministry of Foreign Affairs and the Department of Information. Various other government ministries were responsible for the growing censorship of dangerous ideas and countervailing opinions and thoughts to shape a unified public opinion. The Manchurian incident triggered a political crisis in Japan which ultimately led to a major victory for the right-wing Rikken Seiyūkai party in the general election of 1932, just the second election under Japan's universal manhood suffrage. Fed mostly propaganda the Japanese people and the democratic system seemed to support the nation's mission on the continent.

Eiji did not feel much like some cog in some larger mission or machine to solidify Japan's destiny and greatness. Following his father's wishes, he accepted his exile to Okinawa and Japan. Though he was getting used to his environs and found pleasure in getting to know his relatives in "Some Place Else" there were times when he missed his American family terribly. The letters from his sister Aimi and their frequent little gifts were like bridges between his worlds. Saburo was not much of a writer but the occasional letter from him would send Eiji into bittersweet daydreams of what they might be doing if they were together. Sometimes Saburo updated Eiji on the latest adventures of their shared comic heroes. For his part, Eiji sent Saburo a couple of Japanese comics in return and Saburo worked through them commenting on common themes with American stories. A pale substitute, but the flow of transpacific correspondence did allow their relationship to survive and even deepen in some ways. He loved Aimi very much and looked forward to when he and Aimi and Saburo could all converse directly, face-to-face.

Immediately before Eiji was the task of preparing for the qualification entrance exam for the Tokyo University of Commerce. Playing subordinate roles in the potential glory of having one of their students achieve such a distinction, three of the teachers at his Middle school worked with him after regular classes to help him increase his knowledge and sharpen his understanding of the probable topics covered by the exam. When the time came, Eiji, proctored by those same teachers, was handed the exam sheets and he attacked them with a determination to do his best.

Several weeks later word came from Tokyo that Eiji had indeed succeeded in qualifying for admittance to the university and that the scholarship would be granted. Eiji, his teachers, and his family back at "Some Place Else" celebrated with great joy. Eiji's success was a triumph on several levels, and everyone thought it augured greater achievements in the future for Eiji and the family. There was much discussion at "Some Place Else" that Eiji would become a leader in business and commerce true to the family traditions before its displacement by Japanese interlopers. Perhaps he would be able to revive some of the family's fortunes and those of Okinawa in general through whatever role and position he might earn after graduation. Implicit in such comments was the nascent hope of some that he might remain in Japan rather than bounce back to America.

6

A few days later, Eiji was asked to return to "Some Place Else" to open the large crate that had arrived for him from the United States. It was also hinted that there would be some sort of celebratory feast to mark his success at winning the scholarship. On the next weekend, he got permission from the school authorities to take a day or two off and he rejoined the compound at "Some Place Else". His arrival was treated much like the return of some conquering hero. The fuss and excitement were even greater than when he first got there from America.

With only a few minor preliminaries, everyone gathered around in the courtyard to see Eiji and Kineshiro san open the crate. Almost immediately the "ohs' and "ahs" arose from the audience as they began to realize what was in the crate. There was a shiny new Montgomery Wards Hawthorne Flyer Bicycle that his father had purchased and shipped to him as a celebratory and congratulatory present for his admittance to and scholarship from the Tokyo University of Commerce. It was impressive indeed, though its design was not terribly different from local Japanese bicycles. But it was "American" and that made it unique. It was certainly much better than the old bicycle Eiji had been using. As everyone examined the bicycle, touched it, sat on it, rode it a bit, there was much laughter and happiness as the prepared dishes and food began to appear on a long table set for the occasion in the courtyard.

For the moment everyone forgot the predictable consequences of such feasting and festivities. But shortly the perfumed scent of Deputy Sato wafted towards them through the compound gate and the crowd steeled themselves for his ravenous visit.

"Ah, I see the brilliant student has returned from Naha," Deputy Sato said with an almost giddy smile. "Welcome back, Eiji."

"Thank you, Deputy Sato," Eiji said trying to suppress the shoots of tension he sensed were sprouting.

"Yes, Deputy Sato, to what do we owe the pleasure," Kineshiro san said bowing properly to the agent of law enforcement.

Walking towards the deconstructed crate on the ground, Deputy Sato said: "I heard that some sort of shipment had arrived from America, and I was curious as to what it was." Turning towards the bicycle, "Wow, it seems it is a nice new American bicycle. That is impressive."

Deputy Sato walked over to the bicycle balanced on its kickstand and began to run his hands over it. He patted the seat. "Looks comfortable."

Trying to divert his attention from the bicycle, Eiji's grandmother approached offering him some of what all knew was one of his favorite dishes. Deputy Sato almost bounced toward the plate of cakes and gleefully grabbed two at once. Holding one cake in one hand while he began to stuff his mouth with the other one, he turned to Grandfather Ono and asked, "So all the proper duties have been paid on this great gift?"

Grandfather Ono was caught off guard. He was not aware of all the minutia of the proper way to import and receive items from abroad. "I'm not …."

"It just came like this," Kineshiro san took over the conversation with a guarded tone to his voice. "We will look into fulfilling whatever regulations might be associated with such an event. Except for a little cash from Eiji's father, which we always register and pay the tax on, we do not get many physical items like this."

"Well, you better," Deputy Sato said in his official command voice. "You would not want to have me confiscate this for failure to comply properly." At that point, everyone detected covetousness in the deputy's eye suggesting that he had designs on becoming the owner of the bicycle if he could.

41

"Speaking of taxes," Deputy Sato turned towards Kineshiro san with a slightly menacing look. "I am told you have yet to complete paying your agricultural tax for this year. You don't want to get too far behind as the government's forbearance and leniency to such a prominent family as yours only goes so far."

"Don't worry, Deputy Sato, we'll get caught up in a few weeks after our second harvest," Kineshiro san assured conniving Sato.

Helping himself to a few more tidbits from the banquet table, Deputy Sato turned and began to officiously walk towards the gate. "See that you get everything straightened out soon, I would hate to have to return and confiscate some property to settle your duties and arrears."

Financial matters were not going well for "Some Place Else" but everyone was tenuously hopeful that the family's name and reputation could carry them through their temporary distress. Unexpectedly, Deputy Sato returned in just a couple of days, and he had a copy of the tax register in one hand and a sheet of the importation of "machinery" regulations in the other. It seemed like an accounting was in the offing and the family did not have any delectable treats or dishes to distract or derail Deputy Sato's extractive duties.

"By my calculation, you owe the government 130 yen. I am hopeful that we can settle this today," Deputy Sato began. "I think I'll just have to confiscate this nice, new bicycle and hold it to ensure your speedy compliance with the tax assessments."

Kineshiro san and the others were speechless as they watched Deputy Sato place his hands on the handlebars of the bicycle and survey them all checking for their reactions.

Eiji had been on the edge of the group closest to the gate. Incensed he refused to let the deputy take his bicycle away. It was not so much that it was a nice, new American bicycle. It was because it was from his father. When he left America, the family was struggling financially, and he guessed that even now they were on the razor's edge of solvency. That his father would deploy a significant amount of their income to buy and deliver this gift to him meant the world to Eiji. Though his father was quite taciturn and did not express his love and proud appreciation to him, he knew their bond was boundless and deep. He had to come up with something quick to prevent Deputy Sato from leaving with the bicycle.

With a quick wit, Eiji decided to try a long shot. He quickly slipped outside of the gate and out of sight but close enough that his voice could be heard. Having listened to Governor Ino's long invocation of Japan's destiny and his role in it, he felt he might be able to impersonate the governor.

"Where is that Deputy Sato," Eiji said loudly and with a semblance of disapproval in his best imitation of the Governor's voice. "I hear complaints that he is riding roughshod over good and decent imperial subjects."

Deputy Sato's ears perked up and he began to nervously look around the crowd and the compound unsure of what to do.

"If I find him here harassing the Takaras, I'll have him transferred somewhere where he will have to deal with real problems and hostile elements. Maybe he would prefer to be in Manchukuo on the front lines," Eiji continued his impersonation.

Deputy Sato quickly realized he could not be found at "Some Place Else."

"Hide me, Kineshiro san, please" Deputy Sato appealed in a panic.

Kineshiro san, himself was convinced that the governor was just outside the gate and about to enter at any moment. He had no great sympathy for Deputy Sato and thought his transfer to some other post might be a blessing, but he did see some advantage in helping the nearly trembling deputy."

"Ok, quick, duck in here," Kineshiro san said gesturing to a small shed nearby. "Stay there until we give you the 'all clear.'"

Displaying a never-before-seen nimbleness, Deputy Sato, with the assistance of one of the women, crawled into the shed as she hurriedly closed the door.

Eiji peaked around the corner of the gate and noted the disappearance of the Deputy. Kineshiro san looked at Eiji at first not sure what was really going on. Perhaps the governor was behind Eiji.

Eiji winked at him and Kineshiro san and the others began to realize what Eiji was doing. Eiji tried to encourage them to play along with gestures and hand signals.

"Your honor," Eiji began in another voice, "I was told that Deputy Sato intended to come here today. I see a feast is laid out which surely would have drawn him hither as bees to flowers," Eiji said in his best impersonation of one of the governor's assistants.

"Ah, governor Ino," Kineshiro san said bowing deeply "What a rare honor to have you visit our humble compound here."

"I came to congratulate young Eiji on his achievement," Eiji continued the ruse.

"Yes, we were just having a banquet to celebrate," Grandfather Ono chimed in.

"I see," Eiji continued as the governor. "And where is the lad?"

Switching to his own voice, Eiji, enthusiastically confirmed his presence. "Here I am. What an honor you pay us, sir."

"Don't mention it," Eiji switched back into the governor's voice. "You have done us all a great honor yourself and no doubt will continue to do so up there in Tokyo."

"I hope so. I will do my best," Eiji said as himself.

"So, what is this," Eiji inquired as the governor.

"It is a bicycle my father sent me as a reward for earning admittance to the university and the scholarship."

"Impressive. I hope to see you riding it around Naha before you go. It would be a fitting way for all to see your good fortune." Eiji was in full character and form as the governor. "So that rascal Deputy Sato is not here?"

"No, your honor," Kineshiro san replied. "We have not seen him lately," he said with a smile gesticulating towards the shed where the Deputy crouched in a bit of a cold sweat over the career implications if he were discovered.

"Well, if he shows up and gives you any trouble, please let me know. I can have him sent somewhere less agreeable in our empire to get him out of our hair. It is important that the representatives of the Japanese government maintain good and genial relations with our subjects. I'll take my leave now. Enjoy your banquet." Eiji added for effect.

Everyone was struggling to contain their laughter and amusement over Eiji's performance. Waiting for a few minutes as if to allow the "governor" to go on his way, Kineshiro san went over to the shed and knocked on the door.

"It is alright now, Deputy Sato, the governor is gone," Kineshiro san announced.

Deputy Sato crawled out of the shed and began to dust himself off. He sniffed the air a bit to see if his confinement had negated his cologne and left any sort of offensive odor on him.

Catching his breath Deputy Sato said: "Thank you, Kineshiro san. Thank you so much for saving me. I am in your debt."

"Don't mention it," Grandfather Ono averred.

Kineshiro san thought things could not have worked out better. Deputy Sato would feel obligated to respect a debt to them for "saving" him from humiliation and possible disciplinary action. In all likelihood, the Deputy's behavior towards the Takaras would be mitigated and less offensive.

Looking at the bicycle, Deputy Sato announced in his recovered official tones: "I have decided not to take the bicycle as assurance for your settlement of your obligations. Considering the great credit young Eiji has brought to us all, I think the government can be a little more patient on this matter."

"Whatever, you say, Deputy Sato. Thank you for your kind consideration," Kineshiro san said struggling to contain himself from giving away Eiji's performance through laughter.

With that Deputy Sato, took his leave. Offered another helping of his favorite treat, this time he smiled and declined, professing to be attentive to his waistline. Everyone bade the Deputy a pleasant and respectful farewell. Grandfather Ono offered an old Japanese saying: "A blind snake does not fear anything, even God". He added: "Perhaps Deputy Sato has gotten some eyes and can see things better now."

Within minutes of his departure, their celebration resumed and kicked into a higher gear as there seemed to be multiple things to celebrate. Eiji had secured a welcome victory over the deputy as well as his approaching auspicious adventure in Tokyo.

7

Eiji knew that the Japanese university year runs from April to March the following year. In April 1935, two weeks before the commencement of his studies at the Tokyo University of Commerce, Eiji, packed up his few belongings including his cowboy hat and bicycle, and undertook the trek to the heart of metropolitan Japan and its empire. Tokyo was buzzing with rumors of a battle having been fought at the Khalkhyn Temple in January 1935 pitting Soviet-supported Mongolian cavalrymen against a probing operation by the Manchukuo Imperial Army and their Japanese advisors. It was the first in a series of furtive fights involving the Soviet Union, Mongolia, Manchukuo, and Japan that would erupt up until 1939 contributing to the continued hypersensitivity of the Japanese military to Soviet threats and barriers to Japan's presumed rightful expansion. Beginning in 1934 the Japanese economy had begun to rebound noticeably and the domestic situation in the home islands had quieted down. By 1935, as Eiji approached Tokyo it clearly had grown, hosting a population of 6 million, and become a vibrant modern city perhaps on par with New York or London.

Like any major modern city, Tokyo withstood the wavelengths of fads and fetishes that bombarded its population from radios and radiating outward from the silver screen. By the time Eiji got there, Japanese women were sporting permanents, a fad that had begun in 1932 when the Japanese learned to make the equipment necessary to produce permanents. He also noticed the continuation of the yo-yo craze which washed across the city's population and beyond in 1933. Eiji, himself, had seen a couple of yo-yos in Naha but thought nothing of their novelty as he owned one and played with it himself back in the United States. The blossoming of the cherry trees which normally commences in March each year had already come and gone and he would have to wait a year to see them in all their resplendent glory.

He reported at the Tokyo University of Commerce and was assigned his dormitory accommodations. A staff member initially showed him around the new campus and gave him some tips and pointers about what life would be like. A more formal and detailed orientation was scheduled at the end of the week after all the new students had arrived. Alone and somewhat apprehensive, Eiji mustered up the courage to use some of his "off" time to explore the city further.

One thing Eiji had learned about the Japanese in their natural environment was that they were very private, frequently seeking to live their lives largely unseen by others. This was not unlike his experiences in the Japanese American community that he grew up in. Japan seemed like closed islands shrouded in clouds which enabled the concealment of many human behaviors and realities. He found his bicycle useful in getting around to the different districts of the city though he had to be careful because of the greater vehicular traffic on the streets. Visiting the bright and lively Ginza district, for many, the center of Tokyo's urban culture, he noticed that there was a noticeably French patina to some of the buildings. On one corner there was a French department store and nearby were a few Frenchesque cafes and boutiques. He also, against the advice of some of the people at the university, ventured into Shinjuku, the bohemian quarter of the city, home to students, writers, artists, and a rag-tag assortment of nonconformists. The few leftists who had managed to survive the constricting coils of the militarist political and ideological repression hid out there. Their days were most certainly numbered as national unity and conformity were increasingly demanded in the face of the shark-infested international waters swirling around vulnerable Japan.

After such outings, Eiji returned to his place at the University with mixed feelings. He was happy enough to have the opportunity to get a virtually free university education. Over time he found the coursework in business and management somewhat interesting and challenging. Repeatedly it was emphasized that the curriculum and lessons served up at the university strove to give the students the most up-to-date and modern scientific, and therefore generally western, knowledge and insights into how to build the most effective and efficient organizational structure for businesses. He found the lectures and lessons on marketing were often clever strategies for manipulating a business's customer base. Sometimes he detected similarities between what he was learning and the sorts of information that was flowing from the government through the educational system of Japan and washing out across the Japanese population in general. Over his time at the University, new history books emphasizing Japan's special place in the world and reinforcing mantras about the superiority of Japanese ethics and morals replaced older ones. Books about the emperor's divinity and the duty of all Japanese to worship him and the institution were blended into the required texts for his other classes. He did not always see the direct relationship between the composite curriculum except perhaps to reinforce the desire of students to serve the emperor through their mastery of their disciplines and the application of their skills and energies to the furtherance of Japan's Imperial historical destiny.

The buildings and the classrooms at the university were relatively new and rather impressive. A story involving a visit to the campus in the winter of 1931 by Joseph A. Schumpeter, a world-renowned Austrian political economist, still wafted through the breezes of the school's folklore. While taking pride in showing off the new buildings, the faculty hosts apologized with self-conscious embarrassment about the lack of heat in the buildings as the heating system had not been completed. Schumpeter assuaged his hosts by serving up the University of Bologna in the Middle Ages as an example of the fact that buildings do not make a university. Excellent work and research can happen in modest environments.

The floor of the dormitory Eiji was assigned to was set aside for other scholarship recipients. The assumption was, perhaps, that placing them all together might produce a hothouse of sorts that could help nurture them all through the rigors of their programs and prod them to do their best work. Of all his fellow special scholars, Eiji took to Toshio Sasaki the most. They shared the same bunk rack, Toshio sleeping just above Eiji. Toshio was from a peasant family in Japan's northern island, Hokkaido. His family had been pushed onto Hokkaido by government encouragement in the 1870s fleeing their struggles and hardships in northern Honshu. Basically, the central government promoted imperialistic policies for what was to Japan its frontier region, complete with an aboriginal population. His grandfathers had weathered the hardships of being tenant farmers. Several males in his family joined the ranks of coal miners at the turn of the century as major

Japanese firms began to develop those resources. But no matter where or how Toshio's family scraped and scratched out their livelihood, everything was hard for them. Hence, when Toshio was awarded his scholarship, he was as much of a local hero to his family and his community in Hokkaido as Eiji was in Okinawa. Coming from Japan's "wild west" he was received in Tokyo as a less-than-civilized outsider, not unlike Eiji. For those and other reasons of personality and perspective, the two of them began to forge a fast friendship that served them both as their shields in the strange and sometimes hostile world of Tokyo and mainland Japan.

In the same dormitory and the same cohort of classes, Eiji and Toshio spent a great deal of time together over the ensuing months becoming fast friends. If they had a chance, they would ride around the city together on Eiji's bicycle. Occasionally, Eiji would let Toshio wear his cowboy hat and Toshio would let out yells of "Yippie-I-Oh-Gai-A" pretending to be an American cowboy himself.

They shared their memories of their distant families, their feelings about their classes and professors, and their views on contemporary events. Toshio became the one person Eiji felt he could trust and count on as a true friend.

"Hey, that's great!" Toshio exclaimed and he wiped some of the rain droplets off his face. "Did you hear the news?" he called out to Eiji entering the dormitory. "We got it!"

"Got what?" Eiji asked looking up from a book he was reading while sitting on his bunk.

"The Olympics, you silly," Toshio could hardly contain himself. "We are going to be the host of the 1940 Summer Olympics!"

It was July 31, 1936, and the International Olympic Committee announced its selection for the 1940 summer games.

"Oh, that," Eiji acknowledged. "I hadn't heard and must admit that I was not really paying attention."

"But this is big news! This puts Japan on the same international level as Germany hosting the games this year starting just next month in Berlin. We will be able to show off how modern and great Tokyo and Japan are." Eiji shared some of Toshio's pride and enthusiasm. Los Angeles was gearing up for the 1932 summer games just as Eiji was leaving America. He was somewhat disappointed that he lost any opportunity to attend any of the events, but his family mission came first. Again, he would be close to exciting sports competitions but not able to witness any first-hand since he was not planning to still be in Japan by the summer of 1940. His program at the University, lengthened to four years since he had the preliminary preparatory year course added, should be over by 1939 and he would race back to America as soon as he could.

"Maybe you'll get to see some of the competition, Toshio."

" If I am still in Tokyo, I'll certainly try. That's for sure!"

They then began to chat about their favorite track and field events and the likelihood of Japanese athletes rising to the challenges and requiting themselves admirably against the rest of the world, besting Germany's haul of three gold medals in 1932. In the medal totals, Japan earned 18 and Germany 20. Of course, the United States overpowered all other nations with 41 gold medals and 103 total respectively.

"Maybe we'll be able to explode in the medal totals like Germany did between 1932 and 1936," Toshio observed. He obviously had brushed up on the history of respective Olympic games.

"In 1936 Berlin games, Germany finished on top capturing 89 total medals, 33 of which were gold. That was better than even the United States with 56 medals and only 24 golds. We got 6 golds, four in swimming."

Within a year the cataclysmic events began to explode on the continent puncturing Toshio's realms and ultimately disrupting the future of Japan, Asia, and the whole world. Despite the tenuous truces that had been manufactured in North China to try to pacify the mounting tensions between the Japanese and Chinese forces, in July 1937 the infamous Marco Polo Bridge incident near Beijing ignited what quickly became a full-scale war between Japan and China. From August to November 1937 what later became referred to as the Stalingrad on the Yangtze was fought between the newly created Japanese Shanghai Expeditionary Army and the Nationalist Chinese armies over the control of Shanghai.

Toshio had an older brother in the Japanese army who was assigned to the 3rd Platoon of the Machine Gun Company of the 20th Infantry Regiment, 16th Division. As a loving brother, Toshio tried his best to know exactly where his brother was and pray for his safety. Despite the gruesome and stiff resistance put up by the Chinese troops, Japan's Imperial Army prevailed. Seeking to achieve a quick and even more decisive victory –perhaps ending the conflict altogether, Japanese forces pushed on, down the Yangtze River to capture the Chinese capital at Nanjing.

Toshio received a few vague but reassuring letters from his brother attesting to his continued survival through the engagements and operations.

"I'm so worried about my brother," Toshio admitted to Eiji.

"Of course, that's only natural."

"But why are those Chinese fighting so fiercely, Eiji. Don't they know that they are no match for our imperial army? Don't they know that Japan only wants to help them dismantle and discard their corrupt government and abandon their traditional, feudal ways?"

Eiji did not know exactly how to answer the questions. It was obvious that Toshio was more susceptible to the Japanese government propaganda than he was. He began to realize then that he was in no way becoming a "true" Japanese subject as he continued to be skeptical about the official reports and lines that bombarded the home population about what was going on the continent.

Having been the first Asian nation to retreat from its feudal traditionalism and fully embrace a modified version of European modernity, the Japanese felt that they had a right, if not a duty to serve as mentors to other Asian countries on how to cast off the tentacles of European imperialism and its self-appointed superiority. Japan had avoided the century of humiliation that had befallen China through repeated defeats at the hands of western nations and the forced acceptance of demeaning unequal treaties. Japan had instituted its version of a constitutional monarchy and democracy and felt justified in assuming authority on how it could be done.

Japan began the road towards paternalistic imperialism early in the 20th century and in 1910 annexed Korea with the Japanese Korean Annexation Treaty. For hundreds of years, Japan had always taken a keen interest in Korean affairs and politics. The Japanese sometimes referred to Korea as "a dagger pointed at the Japanese heart" since it was the closest point from which an invasion from the mainland might be launched. The Mongols had mounted two invasions of Japan from Korea. Anyway, it was presumed that absorbing Korea would better secure Japan's national security, and with a certain amount of noblesse oblige the Japanese could serve as big brothers to the Koreans and facilitate their modernization and development.

But from what Eiji could tell, the Koreans largely resented their subordination to Japan. Koreans in Japan were terribly discriminated against and generally mistreated. He remembered that when he encountered Koreans in the United States, they tended to seethe with hatred towards Japan and the Japanese for their treatment of their homeland. He was not sure what good was coming of it all, but it did seem a bit arrogant on the part of the Japanese.

Now the same approach was self-justified and applied to China and the Chinese. Again, his experiences in the United States suggested that the Chinese were a sober, hard-working, entrepreneurial if only on small scales, people – not unlike the Japanese residents of the country. Both populations struggled to overcome the slings and arrows of Anglo racism and tried to be as unobtrusive and inoffensive as possible. He wondered, then, what was wrong with the Chinese in China? Why were they such a bother to the Japanese and required such severe, almost disciplinary, measures? Toshio did not question the government's policies or explanations. Eiji quietly remained unsure.

Meanwhile, in recent years Japan's democracy had devolved into authoritarianism that did all it could to stifle and silence any opposition or alternative perspectives to the official national orthodoxy. The hyper patriotism of the militarists was the woof and weave of the transitions. In November 1938 Prime Minister Fumimaro Konoe had announced to the nation that Japan would forge a New Era in East Asia to expel western imperialists from Asia and liberate fellow Asians from the regime of subordination. The concept was idealistic, eventually imaging the creation of a Greater East Asian Co-Prosperity Sphere which Japanese militarists also saw as forging channels for securing the resources Japan needed to become even more industrialized and economically secure.

Japanese casualties during the battle of Shanghai topped 40,000 and shocked the Japanese public. Angry demonstrations around the home of a regimental commander in Tokyo broke out necessitating the intervention of the Tokyo police. Elsewhere, the wife of a regimental commander, killed in the battle himself, was mercilessly assaulted with public criticism of her husband for the high death toll. She sought relief from the attacks in her own suicide.

Despite not formally being at war with China, both the government and the army began to increasingly rely on propaganda and what they referred to as spiritual mobilization to drum up support for the China campaign. Mass events such as parades, fireworks, and rallies were organized to celebrate the early victories of 1937. A national celebration and rally to mark the capture of Nanjing was scheduled in December 1937 and had to be postponed for three days since the city did not capitulate as quickly as originally anticipated.

Fall it did as the Chinese defenders who could, retreated further west to what became China's wartime capital, Chungking. In Nanjing several weeks of lawlessness and outrageous behavior on the part of the conquering Japanese soldiers unfolded. The Shanghai Expeditionary Force and its 16th Division were in the thick of it all and committed some of the worst atrocities.

Toshio knew little of what was really going on at Nanjing. He was just joyfully relieved to get reassuring letters from his brother testifying to his survival and generally good condition.

"He's alive and basically healthy," Toshio reported to Eiji with relief. A tone of pride and confidence then crept into his voice. "I knew those rag-tag-Chinese fighters were no match for the Japanese Imperial Army. They should have saved their own blood and just surrendered earlier."

"Does that end the fighting?" Eiji asked.

"Hard to say right now. There is no announcement of that. "Toshio said reading the newspaper.

Actually, Japanese atrocities seemed to harden Chinese resistance and the assaulting Japanese forces were never sufficient to complete the many attempts to encircle and trap the still extant Chinese forces. The Nationalist government, having retreated beyond the immediate reach of Japanese warriors, refused the ultimatums and harsh demands of Tokyo. In mid-January 1938 the Japanese Prime Minister demonstrating national pique announced that Japan would no longer negotiate with the Nationalist Chinese government essentially eliminating any diplomatic way to end the conflict.

8

The Shanghai Expeditionary Army was disbanded on February 1, 1938, and its units were assigned to the Japanese Central China Area Army. Toshio's brother unit was shifted about a bit and in the process, he was able to return to Japan for a bit of rest and recuperation.

"He's coming here!" Toshio almost shouted to Eiji. Toshio was almost beside himself at the prospect of being able to visit with his brother, a hero of the conquest of Nanjing. "You'll get to meet him, Eiji!"

"That sounds great," Eiji smiled patting Toshio on the shoulder. Eiji was not sure what such a meeting would be like or what sort of conversation might blossom. But if it made Toshio happy, then it made Eiji happy.

Toshio and his brother exchanged messages and they agreed that the reunion should be celebrated. The designated rendezvous spot was the Sapporo Lion Beer Hall in the Ginza district which had opened up to much fanfare in 1934. It might have been a bit classy for two university students and a battle-hardened soldier, but Toshio's brother was willing to trade on his social rank as a victorious veteran to lubricate the hinges on the doors of the establishment. Eiji drank beer occasionally but had yet to grace a beer hall. He looked forward to the reunion of brothers as much for his curiosity about the Sapporo Lion Beer Hall as anything else.

"Toshio!" Kenta Sasaki called out boisterously.

"Kenta!" Toshio replied with equal excitement.

Eiji greeted Kenta with the proper respectful bow.

"Please dispense with such formalities,' Kenta said. "Toshio has mentioned you so often in his letters, I feel like I already know you and you are almost family."

The three of them blew through the door to the beer hall, quickly got a table, and ordered their beers. Eiji was impressed by the easy animation the brothers fell into as they began to catch up. He wondered if his reunion with Aimi and or Saburo would be as jocular and joyful as what he was witnessing. Aimi had been regularly updating him on family matters, the doings of Saburo, and a few of her thoughts on national politics and the policies of FDR.

Saburo had also sent letters, mostly in response to the letters Eiji sent him. Like Toshio, their relationships had been held together by the thin thread of written words on pieces of paper that flew across oceans. It seemed like Toshio and Kenta picked up almost right where they left off when Kenta left the family for the army. Eiji hoped he and Aimi and Saburo would be able to do the same.

It quickly became obvious that the different paths Toshio and Kenta had taken were influencing who and what they were. Toshio's speech and behaviors were those of a student and a wannabe managerial leader. Kenta's speech and mannerisms were rough bordering on crude revealing the effects army life had had on him.

"So, what was it like, if you don't mind me asking," Toshio burning curiosity eventually burst open.

"What do you mean? Battle?" Kenta said becoming more serious.

"Yes, were you afraid? Did you kill anyone?"

"Of course, I was scared at times. When the Chinese soldiers rushed us for hand-to-hand fighting – that was frightening indeed. And yes, I killed some of them. Maybe lots of them. I am in a machine-gun unit."

What do you feel when you kill them?" Toshio continued.

"Nothing." Kenta blandly replied. "I am not sure they are even people like us."

"What?" Eiji prodded.

"I mean for example when we took Nanjing our Division commander told us not to take any prisoners."

"And?" Eiji continued.

"And we killed them as quickly as they surrendered to us. It was almost unbelievable. We could call out to them in Chinese to come to us 'lai, lai lai' and they would just meekly run to us, and we would like them up and mow the fools down."

"But why would you be doing that; they had given up the fight?" Eiji pressed.

"Orders, we were just following orders. My guess is that the goal was to teach those buggers a lesson about resisting us. To terrorize them. To cow them into total submission." Kenta said, pouring himself another beer.

"But they had given up, right?" Toshio did not fully understand.

"Sure, the city had been abandoned by its defenders and the unlucky helpless souls left behind were totally at our mercy. But the rest of the country was still too stubborn and stupid to accept their fate."

"Humm." Eiji reflected for a minute.

Almost giggling, Kenta continued: "In fact, we had various contests to seek who could kill the most. Two of our sublieutenants, Toshiaki Mukai and Tsuyoshi Noda, engaged in a contest to see who could be the first to kill 100 Chinese with their swords. Maybe you heard of it?"

Toshio and Eiji nodded as they had seen such a story in a Tokyo newspaper, the *Nichinichi.*

"I've got pictures of them," as Kenta fished out a collection of his personal photographs which he began to display with detectable pride.

"Here they are sitting on a portion of a blown-up wall."

Toshio noticed other photographs in Kenta's hands and reached out to get them and shuffle through them. Eiji looked over Toshio's shoulder and looked at the daunting documentation Kenta was offering up. Several pictures were of mounds of bodies all prostrate in the final grotesque throes of their lives. Entrails had burst out of some bodies. Others were missing limbs and commonly their heads. The heads, either separate or still attached to the corpses, all had open eyes staring into eternity.

A picture of naked women strewn about like broken and discarded toys caught Eiji's eye. He winced as he looked at it.

"What about the women?" Toshio asked.

"Ah, those Chinese whores and bitches. They would plead for their lives and offer to do anything to be saved." Kenta smiled and nudged Toshio with his elbow as one male did to another signaling common carnal compliance.

Kenta raised his eyebrow and teased Toshio. "Toshio, I'll bet you are still inexperienced." Toshio blushed and looked down confirming Kenta's assessment. Eiji was feeling increasingly uncomfortable as well.

"Well, it was nothing to dip our *chinpos* into those pitiful *Mankos*. Sometimes they would pretend and comply as much as they could thinking that they might earn a merciful reprieve. Other times they would struggle and squirm – which actually made the event a bit more exciting and enhanced."

Kenta, then produced a picture he had held back. It was of the bodies of two dead women, stark naked, lying face up with their faces grimaced in their last agony. "Here are my first two," Kenta said almost proudly. The one on the left must have been a teenager. She was tight. The other one might have been an older sister or even her mother." Kenta's eyes glistened a bit as if he was remembering a particularly enjoyable coition.

Immediately Eiji felt like he was stabbed in the heart. He could hardly look at the photograph and yet he studied it for a few seconds. Revulsion nearly overwhelmed him. The younger victim looked so much like his own sister Aimi that he was nearly sick. He quickly raised his hand to his mouth and turned away to shield his tablemates from the vomit that he felt racing to be expelled. Terrified at the picture, the thoughts it triggered, and the possible shame and embarrassment should he retch, yet he succeeded in holding it in.

"What's the matter, Eiji?" Toshio said noticing his friend's lurch to the side.

Eiji took a minute to compose himself. "Nothing, I guess it is just the beer. I am not used to drinking so much."

Confused, Kenta said: "But you have only had two!" What kind of wimp are you?"

"It's ok," Eiji said catching his breath reaching for a glass of water. "Sometimes my system is a little fickle."

Turning to Toshio who had taken the photograph from Eiji, Kenta tapped the photograph. "If you get into the army, you might take advantage of some of the perks and initiate yourself. Any and all of those Chinese wenches would be available."

Eiji was feeling a bit woozy. So, claiming that he did not want to be a suppressant to Kenta's visit, he politely excused himself.

"You going to get back by yourself, ok?" Toshio asked with genuine concern.

"Yeah. I'll be alright. I'll see you back at the dormitory. It was interesting to have met you Kenta. I will hope and pray for your continued health and safety."

A fulcrum inside Eiji was tipped by the encounter with Kenta. Immersed in the sea of the Japanese current situation and world view, he had held at bay all the propaganda and patriotic stem-winding that flooded the nation. Within a week of the evening at the Sapporo Lion Beer Hall, the National Mobilization Law and its supplement the National Draft Service Ordinance were enacted by the Japanese Diet shifting the nation into full-scale war-footing. Everything, including the civilian labor force, was going to be aligned and at the service of the crusade in China.

Eiji was repelled by it all. He could not get the picture of those two women or the disgusting narration of events that Kenta offered out of his mind and ears. If anything, it all seemed so hypocritically barbaric given the Japanese pretensions of superior civility. That could have been his sister, he thought – his American sister. And I am an American, not a Japanese. The scales had been tipped and Eiji knew, more clearly than ever before who and what he was. He would remain cordial and his "normal" self with Toshio. He would concentrate on his studies and do his best to push himself to the conclusion of the degree program. Getting back to the United State become his major priority. He feared, though, that he might be sucked into the cyclone of civilian mobilization and become a cog in the Japanese war machine. All his efforts at blending in, assimilating into the Japanese culture and world, "learning to be Japanese" as his father had wanted might have succeeded too well.

9

Throughout the 1930s the Japanese government crafted a favorable narrative of what it was attempting to accomplish in Asia for both internal and external consumption. One theme that Japanese pronouncements emphasized was that Japan was the only true and reliable bulwark against the expansion of the Soviet Union and communism in Asia. They tried to trade on the significant suspicion and hostility to Stalin's regime. But the more common messages it sent out to the rest of the world, designed to curry favor or at least to neutralize any Anti-Japanese sentiments that pro-Chinese voices might encourage, was that Japan was the only legitimately indigenous Asian nation and civilization that had the modernity, technology and will to solve China's intractable problems of political disunity, corruption, poverty, weak institutions and widespread opium addiction. The message was that wherever Japanese troops ventured, they carried with them peace, harmony, economic development and civilization. American public opinion had been swinging in favor of China and the Chinese since the January 1937 release of the movie "The Good Earth" based on the 1931 novel of the same title published in 1931 Pearl Buck. In fact, in 1938 Buck was awarded the Nobel Prize for literature in part based on her sympathetic portrayal of peasant life in China.

There were plenty of distractions, though. In May 1937 the nation, if not the world, was horrified by the tragedy of the German airship *Hindenburg* catching fire and crashing in New Jersey killing all sixty-two people aboard. In July, there was the disappearance of the celebrated female pilot Amelia Airhart and her copilot Fred Noonan attempting to be the first female aviator to circumnavigate the globe. The desperate search for the two dominated the news cycles for quite some time.

As things were heating up between China and Japan, the Takaras, Jahanas, and all other Americans were beginning to get the news accounts of the fighting in China around the middle of August. *The Los Angeles Times* carried front page stories throughout the month tracing the undulations of Japanese and Chinese troops in their bloody clashes. As was customary in the larger household, after dinner everyone would retire to the living room. Kiki would take up some sewing or prepare vegetables for the next day's cooking, Morio would listen to the radio, Aimi would busy herself with some sort of project for the Girl Scouts and Saburo would read the newspaper trying to compare what was being reported with the limited amount of news they were receiving from Eiji there in Tokyo.

"Hey Aimi," Saburo called out across the room. "Look at this," he said holding up the August 27th edition of the *Los Angeles Times* he was reading. "It says that that the British Ambassador to China was badly wounded by stray bullets from a Japanese ariel attack in Shanghai."

"Whoa," Aimi exclaimed as she walked over to Saburo to read the newspaper over his shoulder. "Things are getting out of hand over there. They better be careful or other countries might start assisting China more directly."

"Yeah, but look at the story next to it." Saburo pointed out. "The Japanese Premier refuses American and British attempts to resolve the undeclared war saying that Japan has no intention of settling the crisis diplomatically preferring a 'comprehensive punitive campaign against the Chinese.'"

Morio offered his thoughts. "Those military men are going way overboard. They are giving Japan and we Japanese a bad name."

"Business has fallen off at the stand," Kiki noted. "I can feel people's attitudes turning against us."

"I get ice stares sometimes at the hospital," Aimi complained.

"But we have nothing to do with what is going on over there. We are Americans!" Saburo declared.

"It doesn't matter in their minds," Morio answered. "We look like those brutes and thugs so we must be like them. Right?"

Then in the middle of December Japanese naval pilots on their way to conduct air raids on the Chinese capital of Nanjing, swooped down and bombed and sunk the U.S. Naval river-patrol ship the *USS Panay*.

"Good god!" Saburo exclaimed as he picked up the August 12th issue of the *Times*. "The hot heads attacked an American ship!"

"The radio said that the Japanese deny any such thing." Morio said.

But the next day, the Japanese government confessed to the "regrettable error" and began to offer apologies and compensation to the family of the one sailor killed in the attack.

"How could they make such a mistake," Kiki asked?

"Mistake?" Morio asked. "How sure are we that it was a mistake?"

"Surely, the Japanese government realized that getting into a war with the United States would be a disaster," Aimi put forth.

"I don't know," Kiki said. "I just hope things do not spiral out of control on either side of the ocean. When I got to the stand this morning, I found a sign tacked up there 'Remember the Panay.'"

"What are we going to do, father?" Aimi worried, "if war breaks out between Japan and us?"

"What we have always had to do. Keep our heads down. Be as inoffensive and invisible as possible and concentrate on our own business. You, Saburo and Eiji are citizens so maybe you'll not have too much trouble."

"We are not," Kiki said looking a bit nervously at Morio.

"Maybe this whole thing will blow over soon. it looks like the Japanese army is closing in on the Chinese capital." Saburo pointed out.

Over the next couple of weeks there were recurring stories about the *Panay* and how the issue would be resolved between the two nations. There were also a few stories about the ships of other nations being harassed by the Japanese or in some cases even seized. But there was little reporting from the front as the Japanese army advanced on the city of Nanjing. It was not until January 24th that the first reports got into the *Times* of the Japanese misbehavior at Nanjing.

As the days and weeks passed, it was obvious that the Chinese were not going to buckle under to the Japanese. Increasingly the Chinese propaganda effort portrayed themselves as heroically defending themselves and "democracy" against the fascist and militaristic Japanese. American public opinion began to swing more decidedly in favor of China and against Japan. The Takaras and Jahanas retreated into themselves and managed their rising anxieties as best as they could. When New Year's Eve rolled around and they were facing the advent of 1938, they put on brave faces and went through their normal traditions of celebrating and trying to tease good fortune out of their fate. At midnight they all lifted a cup of sake in a toast to the New Year. They hoped and prayed for Eiji's safety and perhaps quick return to their hearth. Very quietly, though Morio said under his breath:

"Beitan shidai tongzhi Zhe
Baohu women cong
Womende weilai"

10

Eiji spent the rest of 1938 hunkered down in the increasingly patriotically nationalist campus of the Tokyo University of Business and Commerce doing his best to deflect any attention or notice. He played psychological cat-and-mouse with all the peer pressure, public and private encouragement to get with the program and more enthusiastically serve the cause. There were bond drives that he participated in at the lowest level possible claiming that his student status left him with practically no disposable income. On weekends and during his limited free time he joined "volunteer" brigades of students venturing out to do this or that form of public service. During the constant military drills that were stepped up in duration and intensity for the male students, he did his calisthenics and marched as smartly as possible to not stand out as a slacker or recalcitrant. Attendance at various rallies and parades and vigils was a foregone conclusion. Still, he protected his plans and intentions to get out of Japan as soon as he possibly could.

On the rare occasions that he was able to get back to "Some Place Else," he found the compound and its inhabitants similarly tepid about Japan's march to glory.

"They are just trying to do to the Chinese what they did to us Okinawans years ago," Kineshiro san comment one night after the evening meal as some of the residents lounged around a communal fire. "I suspect they will be even harsher to the Chinese than they were to us."

Grandfather Ono just nodded and toked on his pipe. His generation was the last generation that had any contact and dealings with the Chinese. The family's fortunes had been amassed by his father and grandfather who had served as intermediaries and trading partners with Chinese merchants. They had gotten along. And though they had no more accepted Chinese claims of having rightful authority over the island as they subsequently did the Japanese claims after Japan defeated China in the First Sino-Japanese War in 1895, there had been no animosity or compulsion to do or change anything emanating from China.

"The student attempts to become the schoolmaster," Grandfather Ono contributed. "For centuries the Japanese borrowed from China – the beginnings of its written language, Buddhism, Confucian values, systems of government." He took another long drag on his pipe. "The Chinese used to call Japan the dwarf kingdom and looked down upon the Japanese as cretins. Now they want to slap their 'big brother' to awaken him and prod him into shape."

Kineshiro san was nodding as he listened. "It is easy to understand how and why the Chinese might be resentful of the modern haughty Japanese. This surely will not end well for both people."

The one good thing about the escalation of the conflict in China was that Deputy Sato continued to be more or less on good behavior. Casualty numbers were only vaguely reported or made public. Some volunteer Okinawans had been absorbed into the Japanese Imperial forces. Their experiences and accounts suggested the lethality of fighting the Chinese. Deputy Sato, as a pure Japanese, was even more vulnerable to transfer and reassignment most probably to the various police units assigned to pacify conquered areas. Such duty could be dangerous enough as partisans and guerrillas were cropping up all over occupied areas.

Eiji might feel a bit more comfortable amongst his family at "Some Place Else" but he was ever vigilant as there were always tattletales, government agents, and spies, nearly everywhere. Prying eyes had become omnipresent in the homeland most particularly in metropolitan Japan. When Eiji returned to Tokyo, he had the constant strong feeling that he was being surveilled and monitored. Maybe it was because he was part Okinawan and therefore a suspect imperial subject. More likely it was because of his association with America which in June and July 1938 had called for a moral embargo of the sale of American aircraft and aeronautical equipment to countries using such tools in attacking civilian populations across the globe. Vague though it was, such condemnations were pointed towards Japan increasing the burgeoning hostility between the super sensitive Japanese government and the United States.

Letters from Aimi commented, almost in code, on the shift of public opinion against Japan and how that it was beginning to lead to disagreeable incidents for the family and other Japanese Americans. She was dismayed and frustrated as after graduating from high school she entered a professional training program at the Bishop Johnson College of Nursing. Her penchant for service and good citizenship, long nurtured through her participation in the Girl

Scouts, blossomed as a nursing student. Upon graduation, she hoped for a job at the Good Samaritan Hospital on Wilshire Avenue in Los Angeles. She would be able to live at home in Santa Monica and easily get to work via buses. Helping people, family, and others, be well and happy was a passion of hers. The white dresses and cornered hats of nursing staff afforded her a uniform with which she could publicly display her deeply rooted humanity. Adding a small American flag pin to her habiliments was her attempt to broadcast her thoroughgoing patriotism. She wanted everyone to see that she was an American who happened to be of Japanese descent. She hoped her uniform would accomplish that.

Aimi also reported on Saburo's situation. After graduating from high school with a less than stellar record, he, understandably, went into the family business. Through practical exposure, he became interested in the intricacies of horticulture and agriculture. His father Yo and Eiji's father Morio both noticed his potential and they consistently gave him tasks and responsibilities for making the Oxnard land productive and profitable. When Eiji heard reports of Saburo's successes, either from Aimi or sometimes from Saburo himself, he always rushed off letters to Saburo gratefully thanking him for being such a good "brother" and working so hard on what was technically Eiji's land. Eiji promised that someday when they were all together, he would take steps to make Saburo a full-fledged partner in a four-sided endeavor equitably sharing out rewards justly to the hands that had spent so much time in the dirt. But all of that was far away and somewhere in the future. The matter at hand, for Eiji, was how to navigate a way out of the box his heritage and his father's plan for a Japanese education had placed him in.

As if to put a fine point on the national situation Eiji faced, Emperor Hirohito chose to open the 74th Imperial Diet session abandoning traditional formal attire in favor of wearing an army uniform complete with medals. The tilt towards militarist rule and pro-war policies seemed evident. Everywhere the popular slogan *hakko ichiu,* unifying the eight corners of the world under the aegis of the emperor – himself the direct descendant in an unbroken line of Amaterasu Ōmikami, the sun goddess, was posted, published, and preached. Supernatural, spiritual, and secular scenarios were alloyed together piloting the human conditions in Asia. But then, a thunderbolt far distant on the Polish plains propelled the world towards a crescendo of cataclysms the likes of which the world has never seen before.

11

Eiji returned to Tokyo to complete his degree in early September 1940. For a year or so, he had gradually distanced himself from Toshio. Toshio sensed that Eiji was not the jingoist that he was and attributed that to Eiji's being less-than-thoroughly Japanese. For example, after Toshio's brother Kenta's unit was reassigned duty in Manchukuo, Toshio would relate the news he received about how they were building and developing the country and turning it into an economic engine for the greater good of the empire. Eiji showed little interest in such news.

At other times Toshio would test Eiji to see if he might be having a change of heart.

"France is fighting for her life. She'll not last much longer against the Germans." Toshio confidently pronounced.

"Ah, er, a, yeah," Eiji said without looking up from the lecture notes he was reviewing.

"France's Asia holdings are easy pickings now. Any ravenous white imperialist nation could swoop in and easily overwhelm the isolated French forces there."

"What?" Eiji perked up. "What are you saying?"

"Yes, we ought to move quickly to preserve and protect Indochina from any other interloper."

"What?" Eiji again sounded incredulous. "I do not know as much about world affairs as you do, but who would be likely to do such a thing?"

"You never know. Spain is on good terms with Germany, and it might seek to return to Asia as a power."

"Well, Japan is aligned with Germany since joining the Anti-Comintern Pact way back in 1936."

"Exactly, and who is to say that Stalin and the Soviet Union might not have designs on Southeast Asia, eh?"

"That is a bit farfetched." Eiji skeptically screwed up his face.

"Well, what about the United States. They have their empire in the Philippines. It would not be too difficult for them to spread westward to French Indochina."

Eiji found Toshio's logic absurd. "Pshaw" he said waving his arms and hands at Toshio as if to push his foolishness away.

Yet, as Toshio and Eiji debated the situation, the Japanese military was on the move and for four days in September 1940, they successfully launched a large-scale "protective" intervention into northern French Indochina. This coincided with the ongoing Japanese offensive to subdue the Chinese province of Guanxi which was contiguous to French Indochina. France itself surrendered to Hitlerian Germany on September 25th and the Japanese signed the Tripartite Pact in Berlin, militarily allying with Germany and Italy just two days later.

It was hard for Eiji to keep up with the rapidly unfolding events and make sense of them and their implications. All he knew was that he would soon cease to be a student and as an American citizen of Okinawan descent living in Japan, his status in Japan or in the world at large was opaque at best. When the term ended all his classmates received postings to various firms and industrial complexes in Japan and elsewhere. They became the low and middle-level managers seeking to improve and perfect Japan's war production and economic stability. But Eiji was unassigned. The Ministry of Welfare, responsible for overseeing civilian manpower assignments told Eiji that if he were willing to absolutely forsake his American citizenship and swear undying loyalty to the emperor and the Japanese nation, he might be given a position in the Manchurian Industrial Development Company in Manchukuo. When he heard this, he shuddered at the remote possibility of encountering Kenta again as well as contributing to the production of munitions for Japan's war machines. He was counseled to take a day or two and think over his decision but in his heart, he knew immediately that he wanted to be released from the incubus of his conflicting identities. He asked for and received permission to go "Some Place Else" to ponder his future and consult with his "family". The government did not seem exceptionally anxious to draft him into service.

As the accelerating avalanche of belligerent boulders bounded down on the Arsenal of Democracy, according to FDR's phraseology, Eiji made his plans to return to the United States. Back in "Some Place Else" he received rather frantic pleas from his father to get home as quickly as possible and wired him enough money to purchase passage on a steamer from Yokohama. Kineshiro san lent a hand in making the arrangements and promised to accompany him to Yokohama to make sure he got on the ship. Eiji informed the Ministry of Welfare of his decision to return to the United States on October 1st from Yokohama. The reply came merely stating that he had to report to the Ministry of Welfare office in Yokohama at least 24 hours before embarking for final "clearance."

One final scrumptious feast was assembled to celebrate the compound's good fortunes. Kineshiro san, while busying himself with helping Eiji, had not made a big fuss about the genesis of his joy. As everyone was scurrying around pulling together the farewell feast for Eiji, Kineshiro san slipped away and with a smile beaming from ear to ear returned with a bundle in his arms.

"Eiji, come here, I want you to meet someone," with gaiety in his voice.

Eiji turned around and approached Kineshiro san and quickly realized what he was cradling in his arms. His face light up as well as he approached Kineshiro san.

"Here, Eiji here is my new grandchild!" he said pulling down the cloth that she was wrapped in to let Eiji get a better look.

"Wow, Kineshiro san, she's beautiful," Eiji gushed.

"Yes, a good healthy baby girl, a little over 5 kin," Kineshiro held the baby out for Eiji to get a better look or even take ahold of her himself.

"And the mother?" Eiji inquired.

"She is my daughter-in-law Sakura. She's doing fine but she is resting right now. She'll be along to the banquet soon, though."

"So, what is this beautiful little girl's name?" Eiji asked, taking her firmly with both hands and lifting her up above his head as he looked up into her fresh face.

"Mirai," Kaneshiro san said with noticeable pride. "Future. She's the future of the family."

Eiji handed her back to her grandfather and thought, yes, she would be part of the foundation of the family's future. He slowly looked around at all the people of "Some Place Else" whom he had come to know and care about. He had been in Okinawa and Japan for the better part of eight years, and he had learned much both academically and personally. He had watched Grandfather Ono creep further towards his final rest with grace and dignity. At the fest, he shared a few of his "wise" stories and offered Eiji some advice.

"Once upon a time there was a grandson who faced many difficulties in life, first in school, then a demanding and hard job with a mean boss, never enough money, and hardly any time to rest and relax," Grandfather Ono began a story.

"His grandmother took three pots of water and placed them on the stove bringing them to a boil. She then placed a potato in one an egg in the other and tea in the third." Grandfather Ono paused to take a toke on his pipe and sip a little tea.

"After a bit, she took both the potato and egg out of the water and strained the tea leaves out of the tea."

Eiji was a bit puzzled.

"The grandson looked at the potato, the egg, and the cup of tea and did not understand. The grandmother told him to touch the potato."

"It is soft," the grandson said.

"And the egg?" the grandmother in the story asked.

"It is cooked and hard," observed the lad as Grandfather Ono related.

"And the tea, drink it," he was told.

"It is delicious," the grandson confirmed. Grandfather Ono stopped and looked as if the story was over.

Eiji looked at Grandfather Ono, "So what's the point of the story?"

"You see, Eiji, the three pots and the water were all the same. But the potato, egg, and tea all came out differently. The potato was soft and easily broken or smashed. The egg hardened and became stronger. And the tea leaves transformed the water into something else altogether."

Eiji looked at Kineshiro san who obviously had heard the story before and knew what was coming next.

"So, when you are faced with difficulties and trouble you must decide if you are going to be a potato, egg, or tea. Only you can decide how you respond, and your decision will determine the outcome of the situation," Grandfather Ono concluded gesturing with his hands with authority.

Eiji thought about the story repeatedly as he was preparing to return to the United States. He knew he did not want to be the potato. As for being the egg or the tea, he was not decided. He was currently facing difficulties and an uncertain future, and he might have to become hardened like the egg. Being in Japan for so long may have already transformed him into something else. So, the now mature young man was going to leave "Some Place else" having become "somebody else?"

12

Eiji disembarked at Long Beach and was ecstatic to see His father, Aimi, and Saburo on the dock waiting for him. He rushed and pushed his way past the passengers on the gangplank and threw himself into the presence of the trio. Bowing properly to everyone, he allowed himself the rare luxury of embracing Aimi and, in American fashion, shaking hands with Saburo. As he had traveled with only the suitcase in his hands, they were able to scurry away from the docks and retreat to their home.

"Where's the bicycle?" his father asked.

"Oh, I gave it away before I left. It was getting a bit old, and I did not want to fuss with it on board the ship." Eiji replied still smiling with joy at seeing Aimi.

"To whom?" his father pressed.

"I asked everyone at the compound if they wanted it and everyone hesitated. Kineshiro san suggested that it might be a good idea to curry favor and give it to Deputy Sato." Eiji explained. "I'll tell you about our adventures with the deputy later."

When he entered the house, Eiji rushed to his mother who was smiling and crying at the same time. "Ma, how good it is to see you," Eiji ardently confirmed. He quickly took his suitcase from Saburo's hands and opened it up. "I brought something back for you," he said taking a small flat package from his case. He held it up and it unfolded. It was an exquisitely beautiful small bolt of silk which Eiji hoped would be enough for his mother to make something delightful to wear.

"Oh, Eiji, it's beautiful," his mother gushed, and Aimi admired it as well. "But you did not have to. Just coming home is certainly the best gift you could give me."

"Well, you certainly have that," Eiji said as he began to gather everyone into a tighter circle for a group hug. He was emphatic in exclaiming: "I am here to stay."

Eiji surveyed the house and noticed a few cosmetic changes and practical improvements to their abode. For the most part, everything was the same. His old room was freshened up and prepared for his arrival. With a little bit of nostalgia, he excused himself after their large and slightly boisterous celebratory feast and turned into his bed. He flashed through a myriad of memories of his earlier days in that bed, dreaming of being a cowboy, joking around with Aimi, and calculating how to get his assigned chores completed as fast as possible anticipating adventures with Saburo. It felt so very, very good to be home as he finally drifted off to sleep.

Within the expanding boundaries of his retrieved world, many things had changed. Just a month before his return the United States Congress had passed the Selective Training and Service Act which required all males over 21 and under 36 to register with local draft boards and prepare to be drawn into America's first peacetime draft. Eiji thought it a bit ironic that he had narrowly dodged being sucked into the Japanese war machine only to face a similar prospect upon resuming his American identity. His experiences in Japan had left a very bitter taste in his mouth for bellicose bullying. His American countrymen, however, while guardedly watching conflagrations crop up across the globe, generally assumed the posture of reluctant heroes seeking to right wrongs, serve justice, and restore peace.

As usual, such themes were woven into the plot lines of much of Hollywood's production in 1940. Eiji was anxious to catch up on his movie viewing. He was able to take in Gary Cooper in *North West Mounted Police* as a Texas Ranger who ends up helping foil an Indian revolt in Canada suggesting a theme of helping friendly allies suppress challenges to democratic governments. Beyond his favorite cowboy movies, he began to broaden his horizons with other genres. One 1940 film that intrigued him, as well as most movie critics, was Alfred Hitchcock's *Foreign Correspondent* about an American reporter in London drawn into tracking down foreign spies as the Battle of Britain raged.

"Hey Eiji," Aimi called out. "This new fancy and exciting dance hall is about to open on October 31st. It's called the Hollywood Palladium on Sunset Boulevard. Tommy Dorsey's orchestra will be performing, and they have a new singer that some call dreamy – Frank Sinatra. Some of Hollywood's royalty might be there. I think I can get us some tickets."

Eiji had not really had a chance to experience the new trend of swing bands and knew nothing of Tommy Dorsey. Aimi seemed to be thrilled at the prospect of going.

"How can you get tickets to such a fancy shindig?" he asked.

"One of the managers of the band was in the hospital a couple of weeks ago and I was, more or less, his favorite nurse. He told me that if I ever wanted tickets to one of their shows, to just give him a call," she said impressed with her own good fortune and cachet.

"Well, if you think you can snag some tickets, go ahead. Can we take Saburo too?"

"I'll see but I do not want to be too greedy. My uniform may have dazzled him but changing his bedpan was part of my job." Aimi giggled a bit.

Aimi succeeded in getting four tickets. She recruited one of her nursing friends to fill out the foursome and make the outing livelier. The evening turned out to be delightful. And as predicted some stars like Judy Garland and Jack Benny joined the frolicking.

After catching his breath, Eiji began to throw himself into the family business. Attending to practical matters, he got a driver's license. His father was still driving the 1927 Fort Model T pickup. Almost fourteen years old, it still worked well – largely because of how meticulously Morio maintained it. Eiji had just begun to "practice" driving it in the Oxnard fields before he left, so getting his license was simple.

Beyond that, he wanted to apply some of what he had learned in Japan to their operations, both the retail side of things in Santa Monica, and the production side of things on "his" land in Oxnard. His father Morio, his "uncle" Yo, and Saburo were glad to have him engaged in their enterprises. They were sure Eiji would devise new and more profitable ways to run the business – though selling produce at a stand in Santa Monic was a pretty simple operation.

The first thing Eiji did was that he asked for and got permission to go over all the books. Immediately, he saw that things were disorganized, and accounts were not being kept in the most systematic and simple ways. It took a while for him to fully sort out income, expenses, and production costs. Surveying the marketing potential, he wondered why his father and Yo continued to rely on the rickety little makeshift stand near the WPA-built bridge and gateway to the Pier. Though they had operated some sort of "market" – sometimes from the back of their pickup truck in the area, it had always been a risky venture dependent on the indulgence of public officials and police officers. Morio and his mother, Kiku had constantly worked hard to ingratiate themselves to whoever might attempt to exercise authority over their operation. Kiku perhaps led the way in garnering acceptance by freely sharing her delectable delights with those in power, especially her taiyaki cakes. In 1940, though, the changing attitudes of the Angelenos towards Japan and Japanese lurked just under the surface drawing customers away in an undertow of burgeoning bigotry and suspicion.

Eiji thought he might find a solution to several issues. Perhaps they could use Saburo's American citizenship to obtain a more permanent and dependable stall at the Farmer's Market at the corner of Third and Fairfax Street in downtown Los Angeles. That would also accomplish one of Eiji's goals of more directly taking Saburo into their enterprise. After all, he had done so much of the farmer's work in Oxnard that he surely deserved to be represented at the Farmer's Market.

Since opening in 1934 the market there had grown substantially into a booming and bustling hive of activity. Many stalls and concession stands were permanent physical pursuits. A restaurant called Du-Pars had successfully opened in 1938. If they could plant themselves at a spot there, they might have access to a larger number of customers. Restaurants often went there to get their produce which could mean larger sales. His mother's goodies would fit right in as well. There were substantial risks, though. They would have to pay rent for their stall, and they would be only one of the hundreds of similar vendors all competing for the same dollars. They would have to offer the public some unique things in addition to the usual American and Asian vegetables that they hawked in Santa Monica. Leeks could be introduced and more cilantro might sell. He proposed that they increase their fruit offerings with some more watermelons, some peaches, and introduce strawberries and Mission Figs. All of which would have to be specially planted in Oxnard and trucked to the market. They turned to Saburo and asked him if he thought he could do it. Saburo had already discussed some of this with Eiji and he had found out that Mission Fig trees took from eight to ten years to produce after being planted. Eiji thought about this for a minute.

"Ok, plant four but no more than ten trees. We have to look to the future and if we get a reputation of eventually bringing to the market unique items, we'll attract business."

"But that's ten years down the road and all of Saburo's attention and work just for novelty's sake?" Yo challenged.

"That's really long-term planning," Morio added.

"Perhaps but it will help us keep future-focused. In the meantime, we might look around for some other source of Mission Figs as teasers."

The discussion continued and all four outlined what they thought and where they thought they could make the greatest contribution to their mutual success. Gradually, without enmity, egos, or exasperation, they forged their vision and plan for their future. Morio, Yo, and Saburo expressed gratitude to Eiji for taking the lead and bringing fresh ideas to the business. Eiji began to think that maybe his time in Japan might be useful after all.

Finally, they had to decide what to name or call their stall at the Farmer's Market. Again, Eiji had a proposal.

"It might sound a little long, but I think it might stimulate some curiosity and interest," Eiji began.

"Let's call it 'Some Place Else, Something Else.'"

Morio immediately recognized the homage to his family's home base back in Okinawa and approved. He and Eiji explained the significance of "Some Place Else" to Yo and Saburo who upon hearing it agreed to the name. They solemnified their meeting and consensus with a few toasts of sake – the first to a good future and the second to Eiji.

13

The German offensive against England continued. The bombings and dogfights of the Battle of Britain were winding down as the Luftwaffe absorbed losses degrading its fighting abilities. Various plots and intrigues were hatched and attempted to neutralize England, one of which involved the former king of England Edward VIII. To keep up the pressure, Hitler had turned to the German navy to continue the assault on Britain and to perhaps starve it into capitulation or some sort of negotiated settlement. As the wolf packs of German submarines took their toll on British shipping, the British government began to contract with American shipbuilders to replace their losses.

All around them the nation was escalating upwards from the troughs of domestic depression and global gloom. A few months before Eiji's return, as the United States began to massage its neutrality regarding the war in Europe to find ways of materially aiding Great Britain and Germany's foes. Perhaps anticipating America being sucked into the conflagration, the U.S. Congress created the Defense Plant Corporation in August 1940. It financed the significant expansion of the defense industry. Shielded by the continental landmass from the skulking submarines of the German Kriegsmarine the California shipyards began to hum with renewed activity. The Los Angeles shipyards began building their first large ships in twenty years. Industrialist Henry J. Kaiser and partners organized the California Shipping Corporation on Terminal Island and began recruiting workers. Other corporations joined in and in the San Francisco Bay area, Kaiser built a major operation at Richmond, California in December 1940. Already in 1939, Los Angeles County led the country in aircraft production. A blitzkrieg induced blastoff of orders and production ensued after September 1939. The spigot of both foreign orders and federal monies almost swamped Los Angeles and Eiji saw bright prospects in feeding the burgeoning hungry workforce.

The 1940 presidential election was in its final days. FDR accepted the nomination for an unprecedented third term back in June and had a considerable lead in the polls over his Republican opponent Wendell Willkie. By mid-July, though Willkie had caught up with FDR and even had a narrow 4-to-6-point lead in early August. In late October closing in on November 5th, Roosevelt had rebounded and held a 4-to-6 point lead himself. When the ballots were counted FDR pulled in 27 million votes to 22 million for Willkie.

FDR returned to office and continued to try to find ways of assisting the nations and people resisting the assaults of aggressor nations. As an Anglophile, he leaned most heavily towards finagling ways to help Britain while still maintaining the fiction of American neutrality. But in Asia as well, FDR increasingly sought to constrict

Japan's assault on China. In July 1941 the United States imposed a crippling full oil embargo on Japan hoping to provoke it into negotiating some sort of settlement there. Deficient in access to oil the Japanese war machines, especially its navy, were likely to grind to a halt in a matter of months. The goal was to prod the Japanese to cease its aggressions which could easily endanger Britain's hold on India during its most vulnerable struggles in Europe.

Eiji knew little about the complexities of Washington's strategies or plans. But based on his experiences, he sensed that the Japanese military would not allow their aspirations to be terminated without a fight. Indeed, the whole Japanese and Japanese American community tiptoed tentatively through the days and months of 1941 as tensions reached the boiling point between the United States and Japan and public opinion increasingly took on decidedly anti-Japanese tinctures.

14

Undercover and behind the scenes various protectors of America from enemies foreign and domestic had been conducting surveillance and investigations of Japanese residents and Japanese Americans in the country since the 1930s. Perhaps augmented by the residue of anti-Japanese sentiments stretching back into the late 1880s the various watchdog agencies were rather generous in compiling their watchlists. In the 1930s there were State Department alarmist reports that were predicting if there were a conflict with Japan, the whole of the Japanese American population would rise up in support of their Emperor. In 1940 Secretary of the Navy Frank Knox presented his recommendations to FDR as to what to do should war erupt and one of his recommendations was to start planning for concentration camps. By 1940 in Los Angeles County alone, nearly 5,000 Japanese Americans were designated as potentially subversive.

Just as Eiji was leaving Japan, on October 14th the U.S. Congress passed the Nationality Act of 1940 designed to codify and clarify all the U.S. laws pertaining to who was eligible for citizenship. It established some criteria by which citizens by birth might lose their citizenship for offenses against the government, serving a foreign government or even long absences from the country. As a Kibei who spent eight years in Japan, Eiji was potentially in the crosshairs of this xenophobic twitch of distrust. He was not unique. As of 1937, the security sleuths had identified 50,000 Kibei living in the United States.

FDR himself had taken an interest in plumbing the well of the Japanese community attitudes, resident aliens and citizens alike, and assigned Curtis B. Munson as Special State Department representative to assess the potential security risks to the nation. Munson actually affirmed the basic conclusion that the FBI and various Military Intelligence agencies had reached through their infiltrations and spying. The Japanese Americans were overwhelmingly loyal to the government and posed minimal threats to the nation. The one exception to all of this, noted by Munson, was the case of the Kibei. Yet in fact, across the Pacific the Japanese security services were loath to attempt to recruit either American Issei or Nisei to their cause viewing them as cultural traitors to Japan and untrustworthy.

In early October, the FBI had begun interviewing leaders of the Japanese and Japanese American community in and around Los Angeles. Despite the rather measured perspectives of some of the early investigations into the vox populi of the Japanese American community, hyper-hysterical shrieks warning of massive treachery began to crowd out more reasoned responses to the shock of the attack on Pearl Harbor. The sinking of the *USS Montebello*, a large Union Oil Company tanker, by a Japanese submarine in sight of California beaches on December 23, 1941, ignited even further floods of rumors and calls for action against the awakening enemies within.

Within hours of the explosion of the news of the success of Admiral Isoroku Yamamoto's onslaught in Hawaii, government and FBI agents and local law enforcement personnel fanned out across the country and began to gather up some of the individuals on the clumsily culled lists of potential security threats. In the San Francisco Bay area, about one hundred men were swept up in dragnets and held at the Presidio army base there. After five days or so being held basically incommunicado, they were funneled to a federal prison in Missoula, Montana. Ironically at exactly the same time, a newly organized military unit – the Military Intelligence Service, of sixty-five Nisei and some Kibei among the 5,000 Japanese Americans serving in the army at the time, was secretly assembled also at the Presidio and began the crusade against Japan.

Similar catch and grab dramas were choreographed in the Los Angeles area as rumors swirled about impending attacks on Los Angeles or the existence of secret orders by Tokyo for Japanese Americans to locate themselves close to military establishments or oil facilities to enable simpler sabotage strikes elevated the paranoia of the area.

Morio Takara and "Uncle" Yo were neither fishermen nor leaders in any of the Japanese community organizations. Both Aimi and Saburo had joined and participated haphazardly in the staunchly pro-American Japanese American League which had been operating since 1922. By otherwise reasonable criteria the Takara and Jahana families were inconsequential to the American security services. Not so for Eiji. He was known to be Kibei and to have rather recently spent a considerable period of time in Japan.

A loud and harsh knock rattled the door of the Takara home Saturday morning on December 13th. Aimi approached the door and saw three Caucasian men in suits on alert waiting for an answer to their knock.

"Is Eiji Takara, here?" the first man said as he pushed his way into the house.

Flummoxed Aimi stammered for a response as her father and Eiji joined her in the crowded entryway to their home.

"You must be Eiji Takara," a second man said pointing at Eiji.

"That's me," Eiji responded.

"We need to talk to you," the third man said pushing further into the house and looking for a good place to sit and conduct their business.

"What's this about?" Morio asked.

In a brisk voice with his hand on Morio's breast, the initial intruder said: "This does not concern you."

"But, but .." Morio sputtered while being pushed back.

"Who are you guys?" Eiji asked.

Flashing their badges, "We are from the FBI said the older man, apparently the superior, who had already walked over and seated himself on the couch. "We need to talk to you about your years in Japan."

"You are a loyal American, aren't you?" said the second man plopping himself down on a chair next to the couch.

"Why, yes, of course, I am," Eiji answered as he walked towards them and grabbed a chair for himself.

"Given what happened on Sunday in Hawaii, we wondered if you might be able to provide us with any information that might help defend ourselves against the Imperial navy," said the superior agent running out a less-than-convincing ruse for their visit.

What ensued was a tense and sometimes less than a cordial interview, even though Aimi and Kiku served tea and a plate of cookies to try to lighten the climate. Asking all sorts of questions to which Eiji did not have the slights clue of answers about Japanese military organization, behavior, strategy, and attitudes, the interview extracted virtually nothing worthy of the time and effort to conduct it. Eiji insisted that he was a business student at a civilian university in Tokyo. Yes, he did participate in the compulsory Japanese military reserve drills and calisthenics but that was more like the American Boy Scouts than anything else.

"Who do you want to win this war?" asked one of the men.

"The side of right and justice," was Eiji's immediate response. "Freedom, humanity, and personal dignity have all but been cast aside or drummed out of the Japanese military and much of the homeland population. I could never continence the brutality of bullies and the injustices of imperialism."

"Ah, well said," the superior approved. "So, I assume that were it to come to pass, you would be willing to serve the United States in this war?"

Eiji squirmed a little at the prospect, but he would willingly accept the possibility of joining the posse of the good guys out to subdue the criminals and bandits. "Yes."

Flipping their hand-held notebooks closed and putting away their pens, the men stood and shuffled towards the door. One of them reached back and did take one of the offered cookies and quickly popped it into his mouth. No handshakes were exchanged and no properly polite parting. The superior turned at the door, "Don't go anywhere. We may want to talk to you again."

As the nation flung itself into joining a global fight against totalitarianism a myriad of wheels on war wagons began to turn. Decisions by the nation's leaders began to trickle down and impact the lives of hundreds of thousands of people – the Takara family included. Four days after the attack on Pearl Harbor the Western Defense Command was established and entrusted to General John L. Dewitt who was a vociferous voice in favor of forestalling the presumed plans of Japanese Americans to perpetrate sabotage by removing them from coastal areas. Just four days after that the Secretary of the Navy, Frank Knox, reinforced such suspicions by publicly stating that he thought the Japanese success in Hawaii was the result of Japanese Fifth Column activity. Closer to home on February 9, the FBI took into custody all the male Issei Japanese on Terminal Island. Ten days later FDR signed an executive order authorizing the military to exclude all civilians from any area it deemed fit. That was quickly followed by the orders to the remaining Japanese on Terminal Island to leave the island and their homes within 48 hours.

Helpless, the Takaras waited and listened to the crescendo of knocks on the doors of fate creeping up on their abode. In March, posters went up informing all Japanese aliens and Americans to gather at designated spots to be shuttled to Assembly Centers. They were allowed to take with them only that which they could carry.

"They can't do this!" shouted Saburo. "I am a citizen!"

Forlorn and helpless, Yo just shook his head and made a quiet clicking sound. Morio, said, "They can do whatever they say they can. No different than in Japan."

"But we don't deserve this," Eiji objected. "We have done nothing to deserve this."

"I am sorry, Eiji, my son. I don't think deserve has anything to do with this." He then looked at the little household shrine they had on their mantle above the fireplace and quietly said:

> "*Beitan shidai tongzhi Zhe*
> *Baohu women cong*
> *Womende weilai*"

Eiji heard him. He made a mental note to ask his father what was the meaning of the unfamiliar phrases he had just heard.

Over the few days, they had to arrange their departure, Morio and Eiji did what they could to liquidate their business interests. They felt particularly lucky that a Caucasian farmer who owned the land bordering on Eiji's property in Oxnard stepped forward and offered to serve as a caretaker and protector of their land. Eiji drew up an agreement leasing the land to the good Samaritan allowing him to take any and all profits from it in exchange for paying the taxes and maintaining Eiji's legal ownership. They could not do anything like that for the stall they had at the Farmer's Market. They had to just let their rent payments lapse knowing that they would lose their space within a couple of months. Through all this, a dreary pall of dread and heartache spun them around like a tiny typhoon.

As the designated time for their rendezvous with their rendition approached, their neighbors all knew their desperate straits. Looking out the window, Aimi was frightened by what seemed like a mob gathering at the front of their house. "Who are they?" she gasped.

"Vultures," Morio said. "They have come to pick at the carcass."

Kiku was already beginning to think, plan and sort out the most important bare necessities and the few irreplaceable talismans of their lives that they might take with them. "Aimi, come here and help me," she said as she began to unpack some of their treasured China and tea sets. Pausing for a moment, she then lifted a beautiful and delicate teapot and smashed it on the floor. "I'll be damned if they get anything worth getting." Aimi freshly returned from her work and still in her mostly pristine nurses' uniform, joined in and the two of them proceeded to smash relics of happier times.

But Morio invited the scavengers in to bid on their furniture. All afternoon their material possessions slowly disappeared for dimes, nickels, and pennies. Choking back tears, Morio was trying to be practical. Money was easier to carry and not knowing where they were going to be sent and for how long, having as much money as possible seemed best.

One bright spot was that a sympathetic neighbor across and up the street a bit offered to help. Clark Andrews had an unused shed on the back of his property, and he offered to let Morio park his truck and whatever they could pack into its bed in the shed for free. There was small solace in that.

The family followed instructions and with their meager possessions, they assembled at the pick-up location and were bussed to the Assembly Center at Santa Anita racetrack. As the population swelled there over the ensuing weeks, there was a constant struggle to provide even the most minimal of accommodations and services. For almost three months the Takaras, Jahanas, and at one point nearly 18,000 other evacuees, jostled over limited bathroom and hygiene facilities, shunted into eating their meals in one of three shifts in a massive mess hall, and began to experience the progressive breakdown of Japanese family mores and culture. Younger and more Americanized Japanese Americans abandoned their families in the mess halls choosing to eat with their friends at the end of long tables out of earshot of their parents. Eiji, Aimi, and Saburo all dutifully and loyal, remained with their parents in a little clique of their own. Back-to-back they psychologically and socially defended each other and their makeshift home.

Meanwhile further north secretly the MIS at the Presidio was training Japanese American intelligence and translation personnel. In May they graduated their first class. But given all the hullabaloo of the relocation frenzy on the West Coast, as the MIS was further staffing up, the MIS Language school was moved to Camp Savage, Minnesota in June. It came as a surprise when an Army officer and FBI agent approached Eiji at Santa Anita.

Suspecting that he was in some sort of trouble or that his years in Japan had made him a more dangerous enemy, Eiji's body stiffened as the three of them sat in a small "conference" room designated usually for interrogations.

"So here you are with your family, eh?" said the military officer.

Eiji said nothing.

"Well, your name has come up and is on a list of ours." He continued.

Eiji immediately feared the worst. He was going to be thrown in some dark hole and left to rot.

"Do you know a fellow named Hisako Yoshimura?"

The name sounded familiar to Eiji, and he strained to try to pull out some memory of

having met the man.

"You seem to have met him a couple of times in Tokyo when you were both students there."

Ah, it came to Eiji. Yoshimura had been a homesick Kibei who latched on to him for a couple of conversations that Eiji undertook to try to alleviate some of his uneasiness at being away from home.

"Yes, now I remember him," Eiji confessed still not discerning what was going on.

"Well, he has mentioned that he was convinced that you were a very, very loyal American despite your time in Japan."

"That is true, and I remain loyal even today despite the circumstances my family and I are in right now."

"We are in the process of recruiting a class of students for a special school in Minnesota that will brush up on Japanese and learn some of the tradecraft of intelligence work."

Eiji was almost dumbfounded. "You want me to be a spy?"

"No, not a spy, just assist in the collection and analysis of Japanese military messages and information. We need some people who have the highest level of Japanese language skills and unfortunately, right now we cannot recruit enough regular army personnel."

"You mean you cannot recruit enough Caucasian personnel, right?"

The FBI agent bristled a bit but said: "You could put it that way."

"Anyway," the military officer continued, "Yoshimura mentioned your name as someone who might be willing to serve."

"You people put my family in a god-forsaken place like this and you want me to join the army?" Eiji was incredulous.

"Look, this might be a way that you could help prove your loyalty and have some of that credit rebound upon your family," the officer had switched to a more convincing tone of voice. "Your sister Aimi could be released altogether to take a position in some hospital someplace else – like Cleveland."

As Eiji examined the faces of his interviewers, the military officer commented, "If you did something that might help end the war sooner, wouldn't that be helping your family – and everyone else caught up in this?"

"I secretly hated the Japanese soldiers and leaders. I saw some of what they did at Nanjing, and it turned my stomach."

"There you go, all the more reason to help us put the end to the war – even for the sake of everyone's innocent lives, including Japanese, eh?"

Eiji's head began to try to absorb what was being proposed. Silently he weighed the risks and rewards and he only half-heard the ongoing pitch that two men were making. After a little more than an hour, Eiji agreed to think about it.

"We won't wait forever. Let us know by noon tomorrow one way or the other. We have other things we need to do," said the officer. And at that, the interview was over. Eiji returned to his family's barracks hovel and began discussing the matter with them.

"But you could get out of here," Kiku said as her husband held his chin in his hand and looked down at the ground.

"I know, but what about you?" Eiji offered up.

"Don't worry about us, we'll be alright. Maybe even better with them knowing what you were doing to serve the country," Kiku replied. "Like they said, maybe you could even get Aimi out of here."

Aimi jumped in, "I am not going anywhere. I am staying with you and father. Wherever they send us they'll need a hospital and I'll be able to be useful as well as look after you two."

"Then I would be going just for myself?" Eiji suggested.

"No, you would be going for all of us and for all of America," Morio spoke up. "I know life here in America has been hard sometimes. We are sometimes insulted and disrespected. But it has been better than what I left behind and we have made a home here. This is the land of our children's birth and if we are not willing to do our part to aid it in its time of troubles – then it is not their homeland or future."

Morio turned to Eiji and looked him right in the eye. "You lived there in Japan for eight years. Do you really think you, or your sister, or any of us would have any sort of future back there?"

Eiji spiraled into some deep thinking. He could not divine the future, but he doubted that Japan could win the war. No matter what he saw about the unity of purpose, the dedication to the cause, and the loyalty to the emperor of the Japanese people, Japan was a tiny place compared to the United States and it just did not have the resources to prevail in a long fight. Moreover, Japan was in the process of making more enemies than friends in Asia. Its European partners were unlikely to contribute much to Japan's battles. Sadly, perhaps the most loving thing he could do for his Japanese heritage and beloved America combined would be to do his part to hasten a victory for America. Then, perhaps, phoenix-like a new Japan might be born that would exorcise itself of its military mania and discover genuine peaceful democracy.

The next day Eiji made a point of saying goodbye to Saburo.

"What?" Saburo said, trying to comprehend what he was hearing. "You are going where?"

"I don't really know. I am going someplace else."

"Back to Okinawa?????"

"No, some other place not Some Place Else," Eiji corrected him.

"But where? Why?" Saburo was feeling the loss of his friend already.

"I can't really say, and I am not really sure. I have a chance to maybe do something that could ultimately save lives."

"What?" Saburo was lost in Eiji's vagueness.

"I think I am going to be in the army. But I do know that I will try to stay in touch with you if I can. Who knows where you and the family will end up? We have all heard the rumors. Somehow, we will all have to stay in contact."

Saburo threw his arm around Eiji's shoulders as they walked out of the barracks. A big part of his past, present, and what he always believed would be his future was going in a different direction without him. As they reached the door, Saburo saw a man in uniform and one in a business suit begin to approach them. He took a deep breath and clapped Eiji on the back as he walked towards them.

"Have you decided?" asked the Army officer.

Eiji then took the cowboy hat he was carrying and put it on. "Yes, I'll do it." Eiji said as he tried to demonstrate that he was joining the good guys.

"You sure?" asked the other man.

"Yes, I am sure," Eiji repeated with more confidence.

"You won't be able to wear that hat while in uniform, son," said the officer. "It is not standard issue. But you'll have a hat for sure."

Nonetheless, Eiji proudly adjusted his hat and proceeded with the men with a determined step.

Saburo watched the three of them going towards the Assembly Center offices. He followed at a distance. After a few minutes, they came out of the offices and got into a waiting car. As they drove off, Eiji, seated in the back seat of the car, turned and looked out the back window. He gave Saburo a wave.

15

Eiji was included in a small contingent of 60 Nisei and Kibei enrolled in the Military Intelligence Language School at Camp Savage about thirty miles southwest of Minneapolis, Minnesota. The small camp was a collection of barracks and administrative buildings away from any fears and suspicions about their loyalty so rampant in California. The surrounding landscape was a combination of streams, marshes, heavily and lightly wooded areas. Eiji thought it a bit odd to be sent to a Japanese language school considering how good his language skills were. Most of his comrades were equally well versed, though some of them were less familiar with the vernacular of everyday life in Japan than Eiji was. They were taught Japanese military vocabulary and terms. They also learned different ways the Japanese might transmit secret information like coding it otherwise innocuous weather broadcasts. Since many of them might end up in frontline units, they practiced how to interrogate Japanese soldiers in what was considered the unlikely prospect of any surrendering or allowing themselves to be captured.   The conventional wisdom was that Japanese soldiers would never surrender. Battlefield realities and the will to live might override their indoctrination or commitment to their sense of honor.

Physical training was part of the process of toughing them up. Despite the fact that they were linguists and not combat troops, there was always the possibility that some of them might actually be engaged in battles. Therefore, the rudiments of weapons and self-defense training were also part of their curriculum. They learned military protocols, matters pertaining to the chain of command, and the importance of knowing and adhering to army regulations. While there Eiji and the others were allowed to send one, redacted letter a week to anyone they wanted to. Of course, Eiji used his allotment to write Aimi. He could not say much but did his best to assure her and the family that he was alright and that the army food and regime were not negatively affecting his health.

He celebrated the 4th of July 1942 in uniform with his classmates there at Camp Savage. But it was no holiday for them – pretty much an ordinary day. In the evening they were assembled to listen to an address to the nation by President Roosevelt. The President perhaps explained why they had not gotten any time off as he maintained that the real fireworks of the day were those of live munitions directed at the enemies across the vast fronts of fighting. He asserted that the best way to celebrate and recognize our struggle for independence was to not waste any time or hold back in any way in the current campaigns to preserve that independence.

Upon hearing that, Eiji looked down at himself and his army uniform. It was loose fitting and somewhat crumpled offering a certain casual comfort. It was nothing like the more tailored uniforms he was required to wear while going to school in Japan. They had a seriousness to them that was publicly broadcast. Though not as smart and sharp as his Japanese uniforms, Eiji was proud of the one he was wearing. America might not be as precise or lockstepped as Japan, but Eiji knew the mythical self-delusions the Japanese told themselves about their superiority over what they considered the lazy, disorganized, and selfish individualistic Americans were dead wrong. Assumed racial superiority and mass faith in the unbreakable unity and deep dedication to the emperor fueled Japan's confidence in victory. Such thinking had propelled the war with China and now with the United States. Eiji knew and saw all around him Americans coming together to forge the means of Japan's ultimate defeat. Having donned the uniform, he was elated to enlist his energies to that outcome. Sometimes, in his off time, he would switch his army cap for his cowboy hat. Wearing it reinforced his sense of being one of the noble rescuers of justice and world peace.

16

Aimi and Saburo did their best to calm the anxieties of their parents. Word had come that finally they were being moved from Santa Anita Assembly center to what would probably be their wartime "home". Escaping the degradation of the cramped and insufficient space of a former racetrack with some people living in former horse stalls was a relief of sorts. But early in August, they were informed that they would be in the first wave of evacuees being sent to the newly constructed Heart Mountain War Relocation Center in northwest Wyoming. Thinking ahead, the government selected a rather isolated place but on a railroad spur with a depot that would facilitate the delivery of people and supplies. The intention was that the internees could assist in the development of irrigation and land development utilizing the ample fresh water nearby. But none of that was in the minds of those who were loaded on the trains as they were propelled to plains of buffalo grass and sagebrush. To the 18,000 or so from Los Angeles and Santa Clara counties blended with evacuees from San Francisco and the state of Washington, the landscape seemed barren and forbidding. The wind, a nearly constant ariel assailant, attacked them with nearly choking dust as they were trucked from the train depot to the actual camp.

The camp hastily constructed, largely by unskilled workers, was surrounded by barbed wire, overseen by nine guard towers all to secure and contain the internees housed in the 650 army-style wooden barracks for families and 468 wooden bunkhouses for single evacuees. Space in the barracks was assigned to each family according to its size. Since both the Takaras and the Jahanas were three-person units they were given half of a unit and forced to share their 120' by 20' living quarters with another family. They were hoping that they might be assigned the same barrack but no luck on that. As they entered their living space, they saw their new home with just one wood-burning stove in the middle, one bare light bulb hanging from the ceiling and an army cot for everyone with two blankets and pillows. Sharing the barracks with another family was an immediate shock. They soon met their barracks mates, the Nakamuras, husband, wife, and eleven-year-old daughter. Saddled with self-conscious embarrassment Kiku tentatively approached Cho Nakamura and they quickly agreed to surrender one blanket each in order to hang up a curtain for minimal privacy.

As both families were trying to arrange their space and unpack Nomo Nakamura began to get jittery and pace around her family's side of the shack. Aimi took note and quietly approached her to see what might be bothering her.

"I have to go," Nomo quietly whispered to Aimi.

Nomo's confession immediately raised an equally pressing concern for Aimi. Where were the facilities? Seeing none in the barracks, Aimi took Nomo by the hand, excused themselves from the group, and stepped out of the barracks.

Blasted by the wind, Aimi and Nomo looked up and down the row of barracks and noticed a line of women going in one direction.

"Is that the way to the bathroom?" Aimi asked a passing guard with a rifle slung on his shoulder.

In a curt manner, he replied swinging his arm to point directions, "The women's latrine is down there. The men's is up that way." He immediately continued towards his original destination.

Taking a deep breath, Aimi and Nomo realized that the women ahead of them were in line to use the facilities and they joined the line. Moving slowly, Nomo became increasingly concerned that she would be able to hold out until her turn. As they inched towards the latrine, the stench of it began to waft its way into their nostrils. It was almost sickening. When they finally got into the latrine they saw eight boxes with holes in them, two feet apart, for people to sit and do their business. There were no partitions or any provision for modesty. The initial reaction of all the women who found themselves literally elbow to elbow with strangers was deep and painful horror. Nomo almost bolted from the latrine, but her need was too compelling. The prospect of finding someplace in the dust and wind outside to take care of her needs was even more horrifying.

Aimi grabbed Nomo and pointed her to one of the recently vacant boxes. Fishing in her pocket for some Kleenex, which she always carried with her, she handed it to Nomo and then took up a position by her side to shield her as much as she could. It was almost unbearable, and Nomo began to quietly cry before she was done. She and Aimi walked back to their building in a dudgeon of debasement.

The barracks were so hastily built that siding planks left huge gaps for the wind corralled dust to penetrate. Kiku and Cho looked at each other containing their consternation over the filth and dirt in the barracks and began a search for brooms or rags or anything they could use to try to clean the place up a bit. Using sagebrush branches, they did what they could to start the process of making their place more hospitable and a "home".

The first couple of nights were terribly cold despite it being August. At night temperatures went down significantly and the porous walls of the barracks offered only partial protection. So Morio and Gaku Nakamura agreed to combine their energies and to find some way of plugging up the cracks and gaps. Morio and Gaku were joined by Saburo visiting from his barracks which was in the same block, a short walk away. They began to scavenge what they could to plaster the walls. Saburo proved to be especially ingenious and bold in "liberating" as he called it, whatever might help them improve their building. All the while he was scrounging for a bucket, scraps of tarpaper, discarded scraps of wood, tumbleweed, or whatnot, he was in competition with thousands of other men ranging far and wide for the same things. At times he had to run and beat a competitor to some spied useful object. Traditional Japanese norms of decorum were quickly abandoned as people sought to take care of themselves and their families. All the while, Saburo kept muttering to himself, "We do not deserve this. What did we ever do to deserve this?" If he were in earshot of Aimi she would simply answer, "We are merely guilty of looking like the enemy."

Over the weeks and months, the internees did what they could to forge some sort of bearable existence. Even in August the temperatures in the day might get pretty hot and as there was absolutely no shade in the camp, people, especially children, would crawl under the barracks and play or sleep or whatever – just to get out of the baking sun.

Aimi and Nomo would take sheets they had obtained with them to the latrine and do their best to envelop themselves and their mothers to offer some modesty. The worst was when Kiku, Cho, or Nomo needed to go at night. Usually, Aimi would take a flashlight and help escort the mothers or Nomo to the latrine and get them back without stumbling in the passage or suffering too much embarrassment.

As she had hoped, Aimi was able to get a job as a nurse in the camp hospital which opened on August 28th. She donned her nurse's uniform with pride and made sure she attached the American flag pin she used to wear on her uniforms in Los Angeles. She figured that with Eiji away, she was going to have to shoulder the responsibilities of taking care of her father and mother. Both Morio and Kiku were still hale and hearty physically, but Aimi was worried about their internal mental, and spiritual health. Everything that had happened in the past few months had seemed like cuts from a Katana sword amputating bits of their souls. If she could do "ordinary" things replicating anything like her routine in Los Angeles, she might have extra strength to monitor the affairs in their barracks and administer mental medicine where needed.

One evening, Aimi burst through the door to the barracks almost out of breath. "Mom, it was beautiful in a way," Aimi said with excitement and a little bit of awe. "I was able to help deliver a baby today!"

"Really?" Kiku "Is everyone alright?"

"Yes, the delivery was pretty normal. Mother and child are just fine." Aimi reported. "Mom, I was so happy to help."

"Indeed," Kiku said. "Even in this forsaken place life goes on. Who knows what the baby's future will be, but at least they got started today, eh?"

"Maybe we'll be out of here before the baby is old enough to remember anything about their beginning." Aimi hoped.

Almost immediately after arrival Morio, Yo and Saburo scrounged as much surplus and discarded wood as possible and began to make crude furniture for their apartments. Not too long after, they even got some seeds from mail-order catalogs and planted two small gardens to help augment the monotonous and basic American diet served in the mess halls.

Aimi also scrounged stuff – basically fabric and material with which to make uniforms. To symbiotically help herself and some of the younger girls at the camp, like Nomo, she decided to start up a Girl Scout troop. Her first recruit was, of course, Nomo. Aimi and Nomo began to bond like older/younger sisters, which helped to distract and divert them from the bleakness of their circumstances. Eiji had been sending a good portion of his army pay back to the family and Aimi extracted some of those funds to outfit herself and Nomo in spiffy Girl Scout uniforms.

"Wow, that looks great," Aimi smiled broadly as Nomo modeled the finalized version of her uniform. "Our uniforms are exactly alike, and almost the same as I used to wear when I was your age."

"We are almost twins," Nomo giggled.

"Well, not quite, but certainly like sisters, right sis?"

"I feel more American in the uniform," Nomo confessed.

"Uniforms have a way of doing that – helping to establish and display identity," Aimi said as her thoughts drifted to Eiji and wondered what he looked like in his uniform.

At the end of January 1943, Secretary of War Henry Stimson put out a press release essentially saying that anyone, regardless of ancestry, had the right to take up arms in defense of the nation. Following that, in early February there was an effort to recruit Japanese American soldiers. The response of Japanese Americans in Hawaii was overwhelming, some 10,000 men there rushed into recruitment offices. But in the continental United States, only 1,256 men stepped forward from the ten War Relocation Centers. When the recruiters entered Heart Mountain they faced near-total suspicion and hostility. The attitude of most of the Issei and nearly all the Nisei was that the government had already delivered undeserved blows to the Japanese and Japanese American community as they lost their livelihoods, property, and freedom.

Yet, the country had the gall to then ask incarcerated men to bleed for democracy?

Outside the meeting hall where the recruiters made their appeals, many more men milled around muttering their disapproval. "They slap us in the face and now they want us to shine their boots?" said one man. But thoroughly loyal Saburo braved the gauntlet of detractors and entered the meeting hall. A handful of other men were bold enough to join him in listening to the recruiter's pitch. As they left, they were pilloried with catcalls and challenges to their genuine manhood.

On the way back to the barracks, Saburo discussed things with a fellow internee. He was willing to do practically anything to get out of the camp and establish his legitimate patriotism and citizenship. That night everyone gathered at the Jahana apartment and debated Saburo's decision back and forth. Saburo went to sleep decided to opt for the risks of physical death to escape what he feared would be an inevitable psychological death in the camp. In the morning when he was out walking about, he ran into the fellow he had discussed options with after the meeting. Kitaro told him that his father had totally disowned him for considering enlisting and kicked him out of the apartment. He ended up sleeping in a furnace room. When he returned to the apartment his mother assented to his wishes saying that if it meant that much to him, he should go ahead and join. She would take care of his father for him. Saburo had no equivalent dramatic struggle to recount – just a quiet resignation and nibbling fear about his safety. He and Kitaro walked together to rendezvous with the recruiters and start the enlistment process. When all was said and done, they were two of the measly 38 Nisei who enlisted.

Accepting the service of Japanese Americans was controversial throughout the military in the early days. The military governor of Hawaii shortly after Pearl Harbor culled the Nisei members of the Hawaiian National Guard into a battalion that was sent secretly to the mainland in early June 1942. The concern was that if the Japanese did invade the islands, they might do so wearing American uniforms to confuse any Japanese American defense forces. They were sent to Camp McCoy in Wisconsin to train for six months and were the core members of the 100th Infantry Battalion. Mainland commanders had the option of discharging Nisei personnel or assigning them to insignificant and harmless tasks. The Nisei soldiers who were retained in the army were disarmed, defanged, and sent to Camp Robinson in Arkansas where they were tasked with collecting garbage.

The suitability of Nisei soldiers was bandied about with most military commanders arguing against it. But on February 1, 1943, to counter Japanese propaganda about American racism, FDR announced the creation of the 442nd Regimental Combat Team. It was a Japanese American unit with all white officers. The 100th Battalion shipped out in August for North Africa and eventually became the 1st battalion of the 442nd. Saburo and Mitsuru were absorbed into the 100th.

17

By early April 1943, Eiji and those of his classmates who survived the rigors of their training, and the final vetting of the Army security teams, were sent to join the 37th Infantry Division engaged in the Solomon Islands and the campaign to stymie the Japanese entrenchment and expansion of their power on the island of New Britain just north of New Guinea. The Japanese had seized the island in June 1942 and were turning the port of Rabaul into a major base presumably from which to launch further forays towards Australia. Among their crew was one man who clearly stood out in his language skills – Harold Fudenna had already been in the Army before Pearl Harbor. He was as anxious as they all were, Eiji included, to get into the thick of things and start making a difference.

At higher levels, many Japanese coded naval transmissions were being intercepted at FRUPAC (Fleet Radio Unit, Pacific), FRUMEL (Fleet Radio Unit, Melbourne), and or the NEGAT (US Navy intercept station in Washington, DC.) For weeks Eiji and his Nisei colleagues were assigned rather menial tasks at the Allied Translator and Interpreter Section (ATIS) in Brisbane, Australia. They assembled the names of Japanese personnel gleaned from ordinary messages. They reviewed and confirmed translations of Japanese weather broadcasts looking to see if secret information was disguised in them. More importantly, perhaps, but depressingly they collated the reported names of prisoners captured by the Japanese and any information regarding the conditions or locations of their imprisonment. Still, because of residual suspicion of their loyalties and trustworthiness, they were not doing very much to contribute to the Allied war effort. At least Eiji and his mates felt that they were underappreciated and underutilized.

The Japanese naval code JN-25 had been used since 1939 but by the time of the Japanese attack on Pearl Harbor, American cryptographers were able to confidently read only 10 to 20 percent of the content of intercepted messages. With the outbreak of the war, the amount of naval code traffic increased so dramatically that it almost overwhelmed American decryption and deciphering efforts. Accelerated efforts of combined resources in the Philippines and the British in Singapore lead to the nearly complete solving of the code by early May 1943.

Eiji got his chance in April 1943 when he was chosen to go with Harold Fudenna to the 138th Signal Radio Intercept Company of the 5th Air Corps at a seven-mile strip on New Guinea. Eiji looked up to Fudenna, his superior in rank and experience, and was only too happy to be his junior partner serving in the Air Corps the modern equivalent of the cavalry. An opportunity began to arise in early April shortly after they both got into place.

Admiral Isokoro Yamamoto, Admiral of the Imperial Japanese Navy and the architect of the attack on Pearl Harbor, decided to undertake an inspection tour of Japanese forces in the Solomon Islands and New Guinea among other things to buck up Japanese morale after the disaster of the Guadalcanal campaign. Three stations of the "Magic" network intercepted a flurry of messages concerning the admiral's movements and other fleet matters. As it so happened Fudenna and Eiji were given the responsibility of translating and evaluating a message, NTF131755, sent out on April 14th to commanders of Base Unit No. 1, the 11th Air Flotilla, and the 26th Air Flotilla, giving the details of the Admiral's itinerary. Two Japanese medium bombers would be escorted by six Japanese zeroes leaving Rabaul at 6:00 am on the 18th and scheduled to arrive at Balalae Island near Bougainville two hours later.

"Eiji, is this for real?" Fudenna was excited as he handed his translation of NTF131755. Standing next to Eiji and anxiously looking over his shoulder for confirmation, Fudenna could not believe their luck.

Eiji carefully read the message, looked up at Fudenna, and smiled as he said with confidence, "You've got it right and it seems legit." With haste, yet care, they both then independently went through the protocols they had learned and developed to try to sort out authentic messages from bogus traffic the Japanese often sent out to ensconce genuine transmissions.

"It checks, out Harold," Eiji announced.

"Yep, that seems to be the case. I'll run this up the chain immediately. They will want to know this for sure. We have four days to do something with this!" Futenma was almost out of breath.

Since Pearl Harbor, it had been known that Admiral Yamamoto had planned and overseen the assault. The possibility of exacting vengeance on him whenever possible had floated to the highest levels of the chain of command. Secretary of the Navy Frank

B. Knox received the intelligence coup and deferred to Admiral Chester Nimitz as to whether a mission to take out Yamamoto would be worth the risks involved. Nimitz kicked the decision downwards to Admiral "Bull" Halsey, Commander South Pacific, who, when he sailed the aircraft carrier back into Pearl Harbor and past the smoldering destruction on December 7th, was reputed to say: "When we get through with them, the only place they will speak Japanese is in hell." On April 17th Halsey gave the green light for an intercept and kill mission which was immediately planned out.

Fudenna and Eiji knew nothing of the intricate plans. Eighteen land-based P38s with drop tanks to increase their flight range at Kukum Field on Guadalcanal were to be the attack force. P38s had a fighting/targeting advantage since all their guns were mounted in the nose giving the pilots greater targeting accuracy. They left Guadalcanal at 7:25 am on April 18th. Two planes dropped out but the remaining sixteen flew a roundabout interception route, 50' above the ocean, to avoid detection and possible interception by Japanese planes. Four of the interceptors were assigned the kill task. The rest, nearing the intercept point, would climb to 18,000 ft to cover them from any Japanese planes that might be scrambled.

When the confrontation took place the P38s in the kill squad met the Japanese from below and caught them by surprise. They quickly climbed and got the better of the Japanese air flotilla even though one of them took 104 hits from the Zeros. The Japanese escort Zeroes dove frantically to intercept the P38s but could not close the distance fast enough to save the bombers. Both bombers were shot down with Yamato's crashing in the jungle and the second one, carrying Chief of Staff Vice Admiral Matome Ugaki, crashing in the water. Vice Admiral Matome Ugaki managed to survive the attack. Admiral Yamamoto did not. The P38s were all quite low on fuel after the dog fight. One did not make it back to base limping to a landing in the Russel Islands. One pilot did not return at all. Operation Vengeance as it was dubbed was hailed as a great success.

"They found his body," Eiji announced translating another intercepted message a couple of days later. "The Japanese rescue crew found him still strapped into his seat thrown from the wreckage under a tree." With a dramatic flair, Eiji whipped out his Cowboy hat and strutted around the room hands on hips and his chest thrust out.

"Wearing his dress whites, with his white-gloved hand still clutching his katana sword," said Fudenna who was reading the same decoded dispatches. He then looked up at Eiji parading around and smiled slowly shaking his head from side to side. "It is possible that nobody will ever know our part in this operation," Fudenna said.

That did not matter so much to Eiji. He had not fired any guns or killed anyone. But he helped aim guns at a very important target and deliver a bracing blow to Japanese fighting morale. On May 21st, the Japanese confessed to the public that Admiral Yamamoto had died heroically fighting the enemy. Eiji marked the announcement by doffing his hat, the uniform of the good guys, again.

18

Throughout the rest of the spring and summer, Eiji continued to partner with Fudenna in translating and evaluating whatever intercepted messages came their way.

"This is pretty ordinary stuff," Fudenna said interrupting the concentrated silence between them. "Yes," Eiji agreed. "Nothing as important or exciting as NTF131755. Think we'll ever get a big deal like that again?"

"Hard to say. Our job is to keep plugging away at whatever we get. Who knows, something we get may not seem important to us but could be important to someone else." Fudenna suggested.

"I hear that the interpreters interrogating Japanese POWs ask them all sorts of questions about where they worked before the war, what their factories made, where they lived, and what did they live close to – just to try to build maps and information for bombing runs," continued Fudenna.

"Those runs tend to be so massive, I can hardly imagine that any bombardier puts his sights on any specific target," Eiji said in his matter-of-fact tone. "I mean, whole neighborhoods get wiped out – so close is as good as a hit and wins the cigar, right?"

"Maybe, but you can understand why the intelligence guys and the targeting guys want to try to get as close as possible to something worth hitting."

Eiji, put down his pencil and the document he was working on, swiveled his chair around, leaned back, and picked up a letter he had gotten from Aimi. Break time, he thought. She had been sending him letters nearly every week. He thought it interesting that her letters from the United States were redacted as if she might be sending some sort of important intelligence information that might be useful to the enemy if intercepted. The truth, though, was that after the victory at the Battle of Midway, over a year ago, there was no realistic chance of a Japanese attack on the continental United States.

Eiji savored whatever news Aimi shared. It connected him to the family and the states, both of which he missed terribly. Mom and dad were well and healthy, that was good news. Some unspecified controversies in the camp were erupting and Morio was trying his best to stay clear of the fracas. As was normal, Kiku had no opinion on anything political. Aimi continued to love her work in the hospital. She confessed that she did not support or participate in the walk-out of a hundred or so hospital workers in June. The precipitating issues revolved around the unequal and undeserved treatment and discrimination of the staff. Aimi received only $12 a month for her services as a fully trained and qualified nurse. Caucasian nurses earned $150 a month and even Japanese physicians were paid only $19 a month. The explanation and or excuse was that no Japanese worker or employee, no matter how skilled or critical their services might be, should make more than an Army private. The resulting five-day "strike" accomplished little but the "official" explanations. Aimi admitted that though she was sympathetic to striking out against undeserved injustice and demonstrable racism, she had begun to care so much about the patients she nursed that she just could not bring herself to abandon them.

There were detailed reports about Nomo, her adopted little sister. Aimi was trying to help her mature into a more confident adolescent and thought the Girl Scouts were helping. The two of them did much together and helped their respective mothers as much as they could. Nomo pitched in around the barracks when Aimi was at work.

Nomo's father apparently was getting deeply involved in whatever controversy was breaking out. It caused some strained relations between Morio and Gaku Nakamura. But Aimi reported that usually Kiku and Cho were able to speak up at just the right times to head off any serious exchange of words or opinions. Aimi and Nomo did their part too.

What interested Eiji the most was Aimi's reports about Saburo. So Saburo had enlisted in the army and was currently in the 100th Battalion, unofficially known as One-Puka-Puka, which is Hawaiian for 100. He had struggled a bit going through training. At Camp McCoy, Wisconsin they were initially housed in tents and greeted with a bit of hostility by the Hawaiians who called mainlanders Kotonks, "hollow heads", and thought them sullen and unfriendly. Saburo helped alleviate things for himself and Kitaro by asserting his second-generation Hawaiian-ness through Yo his father. Saburo could speak enough Hawaiian Pidgin, which blended Hawaiian, Japanese, Portuguese, Chinese, and English, to be accepted well enough by the rest of the unit. He vouched for Kitaro which beveled off his Kotonk edges enough to allow him to begin to fit in as well. Saburo complained to Aimi, and she relayed some of his frustrations with the white NCOs and officers who seemed to deliberately test the trainees in all sorts of ways – including their loyalty. Aimi related an account of five of the Nisei soldiers who risked themselves to form a human chain pulling several teenage hockey players who had fallen through a frozen lake to safety. Eiji could not tell from Aimi's account if Saburo was one of the five heroes. It would be just like Saburo to not take credit for anything like that in his letters to Aimi. So, she probably did not know one way or the other. But she did comment that Saburo felt that the incident had helped the unit gain the respect of most of those at Camp McCoy and the surrounding community.

Aimi's missive also shared Saburo's thoughts on relations with their Hawaiian "cousins". With tangled feelings, Saburo and Kitaro shared with the Buddhaheads, as mainland Japanese Americans referred to Hawaiian Japanese Americans, what it was like in the War Relocation Center at Heart Mountain. With a few exceptions, the Hawaiian Japanese American population was left unmolested after Pearl Harbor, so they did not have the same anxieties that troubled Saburo and Kitaro about their incarcerated families.

Eiji put the letter down and started refocusing on pairing his translations with some of the intelligence that was being gathered and circulated by the graduates of the MIS working with line units in the field. It always seemed odd to Eiji that often-captured Japanese soldiers would turn out to be quite chatty and willing to answer questions during interrogations. One day he saw a report about that which attributed their openness to two factors. First, since Japanese soldiers were expected to die rather than let themselves be captured, they were never trained or taught what to do if they did become prisoners. American soldiers were drilled in their minimal responsibilities to give their name, rank, and serial number upon capture – and that was all. Japanese soldiers were not even taught that. Then secondly, the fact that they were interrogated by Japanese Americans, many of whom spoke Japanese nearly perfectly and knew how to converse both politely and in the vernacular of the day, seemed to put them at ease. In one instance, a Japanese prisoner shyly asked his interrogator if he could have one of his cigarettes. When the translator gave him a whole pack, the prisoner was so surprised that he immediately began to blab about anything and everything.

Eiji tucked Aimi's letter away in his desk wondering where Saburo was and what he was going through. As an infantryman, would he and his comrades in the 100th be allowed to show their mettle in fighting for America? He wondered.

19

After completing their first round of training at Camp McCoy, Saburo and his comrades were sent to Camp Shelby, Mississippi for further training. They were fused with a contingent of Hawaiian Japanese Americans, buddhaheads. Saburo continued to try to be an intermediary and conciliator between the kotonks and buddhaheads but did not make much progress. Tensions and bad blood arose between the two groups such that some of their officers and commanders doubted whether they could ever unify enough to be a reliable fighting unit. Saburo did not know this but there were those who recommended to the War Department that the battalion be disbanded and the experiment of using Japanese American soldiers be discontinued.

An "educational field trip" was organized for the buddhaheads to try to resolve some of the acrimonies between the groups. Saburo was asked and he agreed to help lead a "visit" of some of the more hostile buddhaheads to two War Relocation Camps in nearby Arkansas – Jerome and Rowher. When the contingent approached the camps and saw the barbed wire, machinegun emplacements mounted and pointing inwards towards the tarpaper barracks, a nervous silence washed over them.

"Hey, Saburo," one fellow called out in a loud whisper. "Your family is in a place like this?"

"Maybe worse, it is in Wyoming! Mother and father."

Sullen, sad, and curious eyes followed the uniformed Japanese American servicemen as they got off their busses and began to tour the camps. A few brief awkward conversations began in both English and Japanese and the residents in the camp immediately sensed that the soldiers were a different breed of Japanese Americans.

"What did your family or any of these people do to deserve this?" a PFC asked Saburo.

"They were born." Saburo's mordant voice replied.

"And you are willing to fight and die for the country that does this sort of thing to your family?" an officer asked Saburo loudly enough so that most of the group could hear whatever his reply might be.

"We did not like it or think it was fair, but most of us complied with the government largely to demonstrate our loyalty. When recruiters came to our camp, I immediately volunteered to join all of you."

"But why?" asked a sergeant.

"Because I am an American, just like you!" Saburo said loudly through clenched teeth.

After the tour group returned to Camp Shelby, a buzz went through the whole unit. Relations among the men began to improve almost immediately. The buddhaheads gained considerable respect for the kotonks. One official report about the excursion and its results claimed that the men came together like a clenched fist.

As they were in the American south that uniformly observed considerable discrimination and disrespect for African Americans the men of the 100th felt they were often on the jagged edge of white racism. Their officers told them that they were considered "white" and had all the privileges of that status – white drinking fountains and facilities, the ability to eat in restaurants, and the privilege of sitting in the front seats of buses. But all too frequently, when they asserted themselves, the hostile stares and detected knee-jerk reactions to their behaviors pushed them backward and away from full citizenship. There was one incident when one of the enlistees watched as a white bus driver railed against and began to assault a black woman who was either unwilling or just too slow to move to the back of the bus. The incensed soldier grabbed the bus driver and pulled him out of the bus. Joined by five other Japanese American recruits, they proceeded to teach the bus driver a lesson in racial manners. When the incident was reported back to the leadership and officers at Camp Shelby, their response was simply to overlook the civics lesson.

Finally, towards the end of August, the unit with its motto of "Remember Pearl Harbor" was shipped out to North Africa. Upon arrival, General Eisenhower refused to accept the troops. Lt. General Mark Clark willingly accepted them and folded them into the Fifth Army. Still, they were relegated to guarding German POWs and other menial tasks. The commander of the battalion pleaded with General Clark to let the unit join in the Italian Campaign. They were absorbed into the larger Japanese American contingent, the 442nd Regimental Combat Team which had also been deployed to North Africa

"Scuttlebutt is that we are going to get into it," a sergeant reported to his platoon.

Adrenal anticipation surged through Saburo and hundreds of other 100th Battalion men. They wanted to do their part, prove themselves, and strike blows against their homeland's enemies – just like anyone else. On September 22nd they landed at the beaches near Salerno and got their bloody shot.

Fear and adrenaline surged through their bodies as they began moving forward towards the deafening din of the assault already begun by the Caucasian units. Caution, as their training taught them, did not eliminate all tragedy as one of their members triggered a land mine and was badly wounded. As the men stopped to assess their way forward and watched the evacuation of their wounded comrade, some of them began to shiver with jitters having witnessed the first blood drawn from them. Their officers directed them around the area where the mine was and, mastering their trepidations, they continued forward.

Saburo, Kitaro, and all the rest of them spent a restless and uneasy night. They only picked at their C ration "dinners" and in the early morning, many of them decided to forgo "breakfast" as they were not sure they would be able to keep any food down in the heat of battle. As they slowly advanced that morning, they could see that the Caucasian units to either side of them walk into the sights of German machinegun emplacements and were being badly cut up by their withering fire. The front units of the 100th paused for a few minutes to assess their situation.

Saburo and Kitaro were in the second line, and they watched, hearts pounding, as their NCOs in front conferred. One man scurried among the two platoons in front and seemed to be laying out a plan.

"The guys on our flanks are pinned down. You guys stay sharp and get ready to fire," he said. He urged each platoon the same way. "All of you, I mean all of you! are going to have to open up and fire at those nests when they start firing. Those of you with good arms, get ready to lob your grenades too."

He then stood up and yelled out curses at the supposed Germans to the front. Popping up and down he moved laterally in front of the platoons daring the Germans to shoot him. When the machine guns opened up, the rest of the men in the platoons blasted away at the muzzle flashes of the machine guns. Roughly eighty men emptied clip after clip in the direction of the machine guns. Four or five grenades were thrown blowing dirt and debris into the air.

Saburo and Kitaro and their platoon mates quickly gathered themselves and advanced a few dozen feet, just behind their mates in front as they quickly scurried to close the gap with the enemy. The concentrated fire took one of the machine guns out quickly. With acutely concentrated tunnel vision Saburo automatically reacted and directed his fire to where the second machinegun probably was. One man got close enough to succeed in pitching his grenade to just a few feet in front of the third gun blowing it up and badly wounding its crew. That left just the one still operating, desperately, and it was joined by the fire of some of the German infantry on both sides of it. But the combined fire of a hundred men or so basically shot away the grass, brush, and concealment of the Germans. The machinegun crew was killed, and the rest of the Germans began to pull back. They pressed them for another hour or so but then they were ordered to halt. Their white officers ceased the pursuit as it was obvious that the 100th was getting ahead of the other units and was in danger of becoming a vulnerable salient.

As the men rested and gathered themselves the officers circulated among them and smelled their gun barrels. They wanted to know who actually discharged their weapon during the firefight. Everyone in the first two platoons did as they were supposed to do. The man who acted as a decoy was shot several times and his body lay crumpled where he had been moved to as the men advanced and tried to tend his wounds. As the officers filtered through the second and third lines of the men, they encountered those who had not fired their weapons. Not knowing the exact reasons for the reluctance, no accusations were levied, but the officers shot sternly disapproving glances at the men as if to say: "You'll have to do better next time."

Aside from the one fatality, a dozen or so other men had various degrees of wounds. Three of the men were in bad enough shape to be evacuated to rear aid stations. The rest sloughed off what they called scratches and scrapes and insisted on remaining with their platoons. The NCOs took note of who had earned their purple hearts to later fill out the paperwork when they had the chance.

Aside from some stinging scrapes on his face as he crawled through the brush, Saburo had survived his first battle. Sitting down behind a little hillock cautiously guarded in case things flared up again, he smoked a cigarette and calmed his nerves as best he could. Kitaro came over and joined him. They sat and surveyed the men around them.

"Man, what a bunch of guys," Kitaro said.

"Fearless?" Saburo pondered. Using himself as the example, he said, "Probably not. Reckless? Not really. Except for Hisako, offering himself as a target."

Kitaro interrupted, "Dependable. That's what we all are."

"Yep," Saburo agreed. "If I have to fight, I am glad to do it with you and the rest of these guys." They both then silently took long drags on their cigarettes and looked up to the sky. Their officers called them to rally and rejoin the pursuit of the Germans.

The weather turned foul and soon they were slogging through ankle-deep mud in the pouring rain. Determined, though, they advanced 15 miles over a twenty-four-hour period securing an important road junction and partnering with two battalions of the 133rd Infantry Division in capturing an important railhead at Benevento, Italy. Saburo and Kitaro managed to avoid becoming casualties. They often debated which was predominant in their survival, luck or skill. The unit as a whole gained the notice of General Clark who wrote to his superiors about how magnificently they had fought and how he wished for more Japanese American units.

20

"Things are beginning to come apart at the seams," Aimi said to Nomo with deep concern in her voice. "I don't want you to get caught up in the brewing troubles," She added.

Nomo looked at Aimi and cataloged some of her thoughts on recent events at Heart Mountain. "It seems like people are turning on each other in bad ways."

"Right, you've seen many of your teenage friends and high school classmates begin to disrespect their parents and refuse their authority. I see them gathering together at the end of tables in the mess hall away from their families. I don't want you doing that. Your mother and father need to hold the family together."

"But they are old-fashioned. They are Issei and more Japanese," Nomo protested. "We are Nisei, some of us are Sansei and we feel more American."

"Right, I get that," Aimi said.

"You yourself have organized a Girl Scout troop, how American is that?" Nomo offered up.

Walking around the barracks and picking up a copy of the *Heart Mountain Sentinel* Nomo looked up at Aimi and said, "We have our own high school, complete with a football team. We have our dances and social gatherings; we just want a little more freedom."

Just then Morio came into the barracks and an agitated Gaku followed closely behind.

With anger and frustration bubbling up in his voice, Gaku grabbed Morio and turned him around face to face. "I just don't get it. How could you not see the unfairness of it all? The government sends us these questionnaires to determine our loyalty when we have never given them any occasion to doubt it."

Morio just looked at Gaku perplexed.

"They have already culled people out of the camps to send them back to Japan. Supposedly they were on some Japanese government lists for repatriation and exchange for Americans in Japanese custody in Asia."

"Maybe," Morio muttered.

"But you know that for decades some of the racists in California and the West Coast have advocated rounding us all up and deporting us back to Japan," Gaku said loudly. "This war has given them the exact excuse they need to try to get that done! They're going to try to do that after this war is over, mark my words."

"No, they are not. It would be against the Constitution."

"Constitution smonstitution! That does not apply to us who are not citizens and they have already shredded that by putting the American born here without any 'due process of law.'" Gaku was getting more and more agitated.

Morio extended his arms and hands with his palms up, "Calm down. Gaku. Don't borrow trouble from the future. We do not know what will happen tomorrow."

Gaku was perturbed at Morio. "Of course, we do. We'll be here tomorrow. We'll still be scraping the dirt out from under the whiteman's fingernails."

Morio retreated to the Takara side of the barracks and sat on his bunk hanging his head.

"Not only that, but your son is also out there in the army – probably shining boots and cleaning latrines. They are not going to let him do anything important. Has he earned any different treatment for you and Kiku and Aimi?"

Morio stared at the floor. Gaku's comment stung. He did not know what was going on for his son. He thought of the saying, "Not knowing is Buddha – ignorance is bliss." But that was totally unsatisfactory. He worried all the time about Eiji. And if his son was earning anything for the family except his army pay, he could not see it.

"And that other guy who used to hang around here and Aimi, Saburo – he's out in the army too. Maybe their plan is to get all the young men killed." Gaku threw out. "And now they have announced that they are going to start drafting our sons. Just throw them away, eh?" Gaku also shuffled over to his bunk and sat with his back three-quarters towards Morio.

"I tell, you Morio, we need to make noise. We need to protest. We need to make it clear that we will not cooperate with them unless they restore the rule of law and treat our children like real citizens."

There it was the jagged edge of the saw that was cutting through the camp residents and setting them against each other and the white cadre. There had already been disturbances over issues like the mess hall and charges of food being stolen. Then there was the incident when thirty or, so, children had been "arrested" for sledding down a hill just outside the declared boundaries of the camp. Many Issei parents were shocked that the white soldiers would arrest children for being children. And now

124

gangs of teenage toughs were forming and basically rebelling against parental authority while adult men were actively planning resistance and refusal to comply with rules and regulations. Morio watched it all and realized that the more heated those people became the more likely they would be branded disloyal. If that happened, then they might really be sent back to Japan.

Morio turned towards Gaku and said encouragingly: *"Kishi Kaisei."*

"Wake up from the dead and return to life," Gaku nearly shouted. "That's your advice? We are just to endure this and make the best of our situation in the hope of something better?"

Morio just looked at Gaku silently with his eyes glistening softly. He still had hope and wished that Gaku could pull back from the edge of calamitous cliffs and not bedevil himself or anyone else with fanciful fears. Just then Aimi and Nomo waltzed in animated in obvious good spirits wearing their Girl Scout uniforms having just left a troop meeting. Gaku scowled at Nomo and shuddered a bit seeing her, and the American flag patch ostentatiously displayed on the sash displaying her merit badges. Morio looked at them both and wondered what kind of future he was looking at. Of course, he hoped it would be a good one. One thing for certain, Aimi surely loved being a Girl Scout troop leader and that uniform. It made her happy and as that was true, it made him happy. He also thought about how proud and confident her nurse's uniform made her. He wondered which made her feel more like an American.

21

As draft notices arrived for men at Heart Mountain, and all the internment camps under the War Relocation Authority, resistance to the draft began to swell. At Heart Mountain, the Heart Mountain Fair Play Committee began to coagulate into a relatively small group of young men in 1943. Gaku was somewhat relieved that Nomo was a girl and therefore not in danger of being drafted. The same applied to Aimi as well, but the Takara family had already donated a son to the war effort, and he was off in the army somewhere doing God knows what. Throughout the fall and winter of 1943, there was a jostling of people and personalities on both sides of the issues. The Fair Play Committee refused to participate in the looming possibility of the draft, but its members were urged to be loyal Americans in all other ways and be willing to serve if their Constitutional rights were restored. Simultaneously other groups of Japanese Americans, like the Japanese American Citizens League, openly and surreptitiously kept tabs on the Fair Play Committee members and their supporters driving wedges deeper into the camp. The camp was basically roiling with tensions and mutual suspicions that were affecting the moral of most of the internees.

"Just leave us alone," Aimi threw a command at the gaggle of young men who had gathered outside the recreation hall. She took Nomo's arm and began to quickly guide her back towards their barracks. "We are not doing anything to bother you." She hurled at them.

"Look bitches," one of the young men began, "You have already insulted us by your high-and-mighty stuck-up noses. You shrink from us as if we had some sort of disease."

"You are," Aimi shot over her shoulder at them as they began to fall in to follow them. "You disrespect our country and the flag."

"You mean the flag painted on the planes that are incinerating the cities where our relatives live?" one of the toughs pitched back at Aimi. "The flag of the nation that has rounded us up and put us in this concentration camp?"

Aimi was caught off guard a little. She did not know how to respond to that.

"If you don't want to be an American," Nomo began, "do you want to be an Imperial Japanese subject? Do you want to be pressed into service by the Japanese army?"

The toughs were a bit flummoxed by that comment. They could not know what it might be like if they were back in Japan, but they certainly were not happy with their present circumstances at Heart Mountain. It really was not a clear-cut case of either-or – but the passions of the war and the erosion of nervous equilibrium sapped by the fatigue of incarceration had pushed people into extreme binary positions. You were either for America or Japan – nothing in the middle.

"We really don't want to take a side at all. We just want a fair shake. We've done nothing to deserve this. All our lives long we have had to tip-toe around white hatred. We just want to be treated like everyone else," said the eldest boy.

"You are going about it in a strange way. By raising a ruckus, you are sticking out even more and causing people to doubt your intentions even more." Aimi and Nomo had gotten to the barracks. As Aimi opened the door and basically shoved Nomo in, she turned to the one fellow who had approached the closest to them. *"Derukui wa utareru,"* she said. "The nail that sticks out is struck."

22

As the months rolled past and the fighting in the Pacific continued unabated. Eiji sometimes wished that he could get into the thick of things, do something at the front and in some sort of actual combat service. General Douglas MacArthur, Supreme Commander of Allied Forces in the Southwest Pacific Area, continued to try to make good his promise to return victorious to the Philippines which he had left in March 1942 on orders of FDR. The major steppingstone to success was to secure New Guinea which had led to Operation Vengeance and Eiji's participation in the killing of Admiral Yamamoto. The campaign to clear New Guinea of Japanese forces consumed the rest of 1943 and spilled over into 1944. That meant that Eiji and Harold Fudenna stayed largely in place and continued their work.

He heard rumors that some of his classmates and other Military Intelligence Service Language School graduates had been assigned to assist long-range jungle penetration operations in Burma in a unit commanded by General Frank Merrill. He envied the excitement and adventure they were likely to have. Operating behind enemy lines in the jungle, they might even have the opportunity to use their Japanese to disrupt things and confuse Japanese soldiers by shouting out contradictory commands to them or patching into radio communications and putting out false information. He was sure he could use his voice skills to do that. But such was not the case.

The letters from Aimi kept him appraised of the turmoil at Heart Mountain and to some degree the exploits of Saburo. He certainly was getting into the thick of things in the Italian campaign. He had been promoted all the way up to buck sergeant. That meant he actually outranked Eiji who seemed to be frozen in the rank of corporal. That did not bother Eiji though as he was more focused on just doing his job as well as he could. Eiji did what he could to tap army sources and information about the movements of the 100th Battalion. He rattled the tree of rumors as best he could but that generally did not provide much news either. Spotty information only whetted his appetite further and fueled his imagination with fears for Saburo's safety.   By January 1944 the pace of things in both Europe and Asia had picked up considerably and Eiji had the premonition of bigger things ahead for himself and Saburo.

23

In mid-January 1944 the 100th Battalion, part of the 34th Infantry Division, helped spearhead the first two assaults on the heavily fortified German defenses – the Gustav Line -- anchored by a monastery and fortress atop of Monte Cassino.

"God, it's dark," Saburo whispered to Kitaro. "Hopefully they won't see us." He said, nodding forward to the walls they were approaching as quietly as possible.

"Let's hope so." Kitaro agreed.

They were in company A which was on the left, while company B, covered with smoke, was in the middle, and C company was on the right. The wind began to blow away the smokescreen and suddenly the German machineguns let go with their hot lead dispensers of death. The hail of fire shredded the foliage next to Saburo and Kitaro as they flattened for as much cover as they could get. They saw through the corner of their eyes Company B's men cut down. The one closest to them got hit in the stomach. It immediately erupted expelling a pinkish tangled glob of intestines. Saburo and Kitaro had never seen anything like that; intestines stored in the body under pressure popping out when the stomach is punctured.

The machinegun fire continued, and more and more men were killed and wounded. Initially, Saburo and Kitaro were seemingly safe in their position, and they began to return fire. But by doing that they called attention to where they were, and soon German guns were turned on them. They faced the soldier-under-fire's constant dilemma – to move or not to move. They had not been hit yet but it might only be a matter of time. Moving could expose them but also, they might reposition themselves in a safer spot. Then again, maybe not.

"Come on, better move," Kitaro shouted. The noise of the battle was almost deafening, but Saburo knew what was said and what they had to do. Leaping up they went forward at angles a few paces and dropped down again. Saburo went to the left and Kitaro went to the right, increasing the distance between them. Better that one of them get hit than both, they simultaneously and instinctively thought.

Throughout the night the men of the 100th Battalion inched forward with dogged determination. The killing let up intermittently as the Germans reloaded and repositioned themselves somewhat to achieve better vantage points. This fight was not like the first one they were in where the concentration of their fire successfully knocked out German machineguns in the woods. For the most part, the Germans were behind ten-foot-thick walls and most of Saburo's and Kitaro's hurried fire just chipped the walls near the gun portholes. As company B approached the wall it had been reduced to only fourteen of its original 187 men. Saburo looked on in awe as they continued to fight and cringed as he scanned the field of bodies they had left behind. As dawn broke it was clear that the three companies of the 100th were broken. They had held their ground all night long but were decimated in the process. They were pulled back to San Micheli regroup.

During the respite, Saburo and the rest of the battalion took stock of their situation. Amazed that he did not have a scratch on him, he joked with Kitaro that he was invisible. Kitaro was nursing a minorly twisted wrist which he got catching his fall as he flung himself to the ground at one point. He shrugged it off and tested it out to make sure he could use his hand sufficiently if and when they were thrown into the breach again.

"Yes, they can't see me. That's the only explanation I have." Saburo kidded.

"I would not put much faith in that theory," Kitaro laughed a bit. "Maybe they were just bad shots."

Looking at the remnants of their unit, poor marksmanship did not seem to be in evidence. The companies were reorganized, and the few survivors of company B were folded into company A.

On February 8th they were ordered to assault the Germans again and take Castile Hill. Again, they suffered badly but succeeded in taking the hill and holding it for four days against machineguns and German tanks. But the rest of the 34th on its left flank was pushed back and the 100th retreated for a second time. Catching their breath for only a little bit, they were again thrown against the German defenders. One platoon was shrunk from 40 to 5. Such losses lead to another pullout.

"See, I am invisible," Saburo continued to maintain with Kitaro. Kitaro still did not accept Saburo's theory. Nonetheless, they were gratefully amazed at their continued good fortune when so many of their comrades had been wounded or killed. Back in San Micheli for rest and reorganization, they began to receive replacements. In the five months of fighting in Italy, the original force of 1,300 men had been reduced to 500. In the back of their minds, both Saburo and Kitaro guessed that there might be a statistical time clock and that it might be only a matter of time before Saburo ceased to be invisible and Kitaro stopped being just plain lucky.

24

By the beginning of 1944, Eiji had left his station in New Guinea working with Harold Fudenna and been reassigned to interception, translation, and intelligence evaluation in Brisbane, Australia. Eiji was still getting used to the weather patterns in the southern hemisphere. The summer of 1944 in Brisbane, was beginning to taper off in February and autumn tiptoed in in March – usually the wettest month of the year. His situation there was tenuous and vulnerable. Not only did he have to deal with continued low-level suspicion from nearly all sides due to his race but in general American servicemen and Australian servicemen had been at odds ever since the Battle of Brisbane in November 1942. Several interconnected resentments and rancor had effloresced between the American and Australian warriors erupting into two days of rioting on November 26-27th leaving one Aussie dead and hundreds of servicemen on both sides injured, battered, and bruised. Due to censorship on both sides, no real accurate account of what happened ever reached the public and the only thing Eiji knew of it was the rumors that had been passed on to him after his arrival cautioning him to be very careful around Aussie soldiers and the Aussies in general. Such cautionary warnings seemed warranted as riotous confrontations continued to break out in places like Melbourne, Bondi, and Perth through 1942 and 1944. Most recently, Eiji and the rest of the American contingent in Australia learned of a rumble in Fremantle in April 1944.

To counteract the dull throb of vulnerability that shadowed him, Eiji kept the company of the small group of Nisei he was working with or simply sought safety in solitude. In many ways, it reminded him of some of what he endured while going to school in Tokyo, with relatively few friends and none like Toshio Sasaki who had been his pal for much of his time at the University. He took great solace in Aimi's letters though the news from Heart Mountain camp was troublesome in many ways. News of Saburo, relayed from Aimi, was always weeks old. He did receive a heavily redacted letter from Saburo himself with no real details of his situation save his complaints about the sorts of things that all GIs complain about – mostly the food and KP details. Eiji really had to guess and extrapolate what might be going on from the general news he received about the Italian campaign. He kept his eye on the ball and the goal of speeding up the end of the war for everyone by doing his share of translation and intelligence assessment like he had for a year. What he did not know was what was a twist of fate further north as the US navy was slugging its way towards the Marianas Islands would recruit him for significant service again.

The successful murder of Admiral Yamamoto had triggered staff changes in the Imperial navy. Admiral Koga Mineichi succeeded Yamamoto as Commander in Chief of the Combined Fleet and Vice Admiral Shigeru Fukudome was his Chief of Staff. On March 31, while coordinating the retreat of the Combined Fleet from Palau to the southern Philippines the two admirals left Palau in separate planes to fly to Davao. They encountered a typhoon which caused both planes to crash. Admiral Mineichi did not survive but Vice Admiral Shigeru's plane ditched in the water, and he did. After hours in the water, he was spotted by some Filipino fishermen who plucked him from the sea and retrieved a briefcase containing a Japanese battle plan -- Operation Z. The fishermen turned him over to Filipino guerillas led by an American officer. The Vice-Admiral was subsequently released to prevent the possibility of reprisals against Filipino or Americans in Japanese hands. But the plans, in plain text, were rushed through American linkages and eventually by submarine to Australia. Finally, they were delivered to Brisbane and the team of translators that included Eiji.

Suddenly Eiji was in the thick of things again. His mind and body tingled as if electricity rather than blood was surging through his veins. There was no logical explanation as to why the plans were in plain text – which was rather easily translated. It was possible that they were a ruse to disguise the Japanese navy's real intentions. But Eiji and his colleagues carefully evaluated the text for its similarities to known, coded, texts and decided that the similarities were such that Operation Z seemed like the real thing.

Copies of the translated texts were immediately dispatched to General Douglas MacArthur who rushed them to Admiral Chester Nimitz, Commander in Chief of the Pacific Fleet. The plans revealed the Japanese offensive strategy in defending the Marianas Islands, and especially Saipan, from an impending American invasion. Aware of both the diversionary feints and the planned main thrusts, Admiral Nimitz was able to devise essentially an ambush for the Japanese navy to coincide with the amphibious landings on Saipan.

For two days in June, the largest carrier-versus-carrier battle involving twenty-four aircraft carriers raged. American pilots forewarned as to where the Japanese were going to be and where their planes would attack from maneuvered themselves into the most advantageous positions and perpetrated what they called the Great Marianas Turkey Shoot. It was a smashing victory for the Americans losing 126 aircraft and 109 casualties to over 600 Japanese planes destroyed, three fleet carriers sunk, and almost 3,000 Japanese casualties.

Reports of the battle were closely followed by Eiji who wore his cowboy hat in celebration for a week after the battle. Hungry for possible eyewitness and participant accounts, for several weeks thereafter he slipped out of his secure bubble of his few friends and associates and ventured into the pubs and bars known to be frequented by American airmen on leave from the front. Disappointed at never connecting with any, Eiji had to reassure himself that indirectly he had done his uniformed part as a member of the huge American posse riding to the rescue of the peoples and lands overrun and threatened by the Imperial forces of Japan.

25

Saburo and Kitaro and the remnants of the 100th Battalion did not get a very long rest. The reorganized and repopulated 100th was ordered into the breach at the Anzio beachhead at the end of March. The fighting there more resembled a World War I style trench engagement with a broad and wide "no man's land" separating the opposing forces. Probing forays were made of enemy defenses at night. Days were spent sleeping preparing for the next night's engagements.   For nearly 63 days the 100th primarily sat in foxholes waiting for some movement in the line or their opportunity to attack. Saburo and Kitaro found it all nerve-wracking and tedious but perhaps preferable to charging machinegun nests.

But at the end of May, a major effort was made to roll the Germans up and push them north out of Italy. The Allies were picking up momentum and pushing on towards Rome. Dependably, the 100th was given the task of clearing the last heavy German resistance about a dozen miles south of Rome. It was another very tough fight and both Saburo and Kitaro came close to buying the farm a couple of times. But luck was with them and Saburo became even more convinced that he was invisible.

"Christ!" Saburo shouted. "Those sons of bitches!"

"What?" asked Kitaro.

"Captain just told me that we are to bivouac here for a couple of days," Saburo said with a sour look on his face. "Rome is just ten miles down the road and we've cleared the road to it. It would be a cakewalk now."

As they were distributing their gear and finding a good place to make their "bed" they watched other Caucasian elements of the Division begin to march past them towards Rome.

"They'll get to Rome before us," Kitaro protested.

"That's right," Saburo affirmed. "And they'll get the credit for 'liberating Rome.'"

"But why?" asked Kitaro.

A certain kind of pain wrinkled Saburo's face as he paused what he was doing and watched. Soon all the rest of the survivors of the 100th were watching with their mouths open and their shoulders slumping.

"Because they are white," Saburo said through clenched teeth. "They want to make sure that "white" Rome gets saved by "white" Americans. It's only the sporting thing to do –right?"

Another member of the 100th with blood all over his uniform from a comrade he cradled as he died of wounds walked towards the marching men pulling his uniform out as if to offer it to them.

"Hey, want to look like you've earned the victory?" the fellow asked. "Here take it. Your uniforms are too clean and pristine to be liberators."

The whole 100th grumbled and groused. Theories about racism and the motivations of their commanding offices were thrown from foxhole to foxhole over the improvised fires heating water for the little bit of coffee some of them had preserved.

They watched and wondered if they were ever going to see Rome at all. After six days "guarding" the road that was not threatened by anything but perhaps rainwater – they were packed up and moved to Civitavecchia, a suburban district of Rome. They got close and could see parts of Rome from where they were encamped. But the glory and the celebrations and the gratitude of the Romans had all been directed to others. It was at Civitavecchia that the undermanned 100th was replenished by the arrival of the 442nd Regimental Combat Team. They were an almost exclusively

Hawaiian Nisei unit created by presidential orders back in 1943. They had left the United States in April 1944 were just catching up with the shredded 100th Battalion. The two units were fused together and because of its combat record and well-recognized heroism, the hybrid unit became the 100th/442nd Regimental Combat Team under the 34th Division. Saburo, Kitaro, and the veterans of the 100th were happy to keep their identity, and the two groups of men quickly fused to become an exceptional fighting force. Saburo just wanted to remain "invisible" and Kitaro who tried his best to stay close to Saburo hoped that whatever good fortune his brother-in-arms had would extend to him as well.

26

Aimi's letters recounted the flow of time and events at Heart Mountain through the end of 1943 and well into 1944. Some of the monotony was alleviated by the activities of the Heart Mountain high school. In the fall, they fielded a football team and though they were not permitted to go to other schools, local teams were permitted to enter the camp for the games. Aimi and Nomo made it a point to go to the games and cheer on the Heart Mountain Eagles. The Eagles were spectacularly good, winning all their six games in the fall of 1943 trouncing their opponents by a combined score of 137 to 0. Christmas and the holidays had come and gone in the camp and Aimi, Morio, and Kiku had spruced up their quarters a bit and exchanged little gifts they had purchased with their wages. On passes they had gotten to shop in Cody and Powell, Wyoming. Morio had worked briefly at the camp sawmill for $12 a month but when the opportunity presented itself, he volunteered to do agricultural work on some of the surrounding farms outside the camp. He made more money doing that and he certainly enjoyed getting out of their stark commorancy. "Uncle" Yo was on the same work details as Morio so their ventures beyond the barbed wire were also opportunities for them to enjoy each other's company.

Gaku initially joined the crew that worked on the Heart Mountain Canal waterproofing it with tons of bentonite. But as he had become more and more dissatisfied with being an innocent prisoner, he withdrew from the details and stopped cooperating with any camp policy unless it was absolutely necessary. That meant that he and Cho and Nomo lived a much more Spartan existence beside the Takaras. Kiku and Aimi, even Morio, did what they could to soften the effect of Gaku's obstinacy.

As time went by, the Caucasian friend and care keeper of Eiji's land near Oxnard ceased to communicate with them or send even a pittance of the profits he was making from the land. Appeals to him to explain what was going on began come back to them marked "Return to Sender." Aimi failed to mention any of this in her letters to Eiji because she did not want to worry him about a situation that was opaque and mysterious. There was the slowly disintegrating hope that it was all a misunderstanding and that when the family was able to leave the camp and return to the Los Angeles area, things could be sorted out.

"Things have really begun to heat up, "Aimi wrote in one letter at the beginning of March. "As you might know, the government has reclassified our Nisei males as eligible for the draft. The Fair Play Committee has stepped up its protests. On March 1st nearly 400 people attended one of their public rallies."

Eiji had volunteered and therefore he had mixed feelings about draft resisters. He fully understood the resentments that could inspire their recalcitrance. But then he also saw the value of everyone who could contribute to the shortening of the war through service.

"Then the Committee announced that they intended to refuse to take draft physicals and urged their supporters to do the same," Aimi reported. "A couple of days after that a couple of potential draftees refused and within a week, they were joined by ten others," the letter continued. "The camp newspaper published editorials and letters denouncing the refusers as did the Japanese American League. I am trying to stay as neutral as possible while still supporting you, dear brother."

He got another letter just two days later. Aimi told him that at the end of March U.S. Marshals entered the camp and arrested twelve of the draft resisters in the camp. They were taken out of

140

the camp. "They are in jails now. How ironic, depriving people of their freedom who had already been deprived of it," Aimi commented. One of the leaders of the Committee was also pulled from the camp. "Rumor is that he's been sent to Tule Lake in California, but nobody knows for sure yet."

News about Saburo was sparse and cryptic. Aimi merely forward his attestation of surviving the battles and how brave his comrades all were in fighting the good fight – crusading against German haughtiness and racism. Saburo asked about Eiji in his letters and Aimi admitted that she did not have much to share about her brother – except that he was in Australia, to which Saburo wryly commented once, "It must be tough."

27

After only a couple of days' rest, Saburo, Kitaro and the remaining veterans of the 100th Battalion incorporated into the 442nd Combat Team continued assaulting German positions in Italy. During the attack on Belvedere in Tuscany, Companies A, B, and C were engaged in a flanking operation blocking the German escape from the frontal assault on the town by the 442nd. As the Germans attempted a hasty retreat, they crashed right into the positions that Saburo and Kitaro were holding. During the firefight, Saburo shot several German soldiers and repelled the fierce fighting of desperate men. One man, out of ammunition, tried to plow through the line and ran at Saburo with his bayonetted rifle. Saburo hesitated a second or two, shocked almost at the insanity in the man's eyes. Quickly he refocused and shot the man in his torso. Still, he stumbled on and Saburo shot him twice more.

His heart was pounding, and his nerves were tingling, but he had no time for anything like reflective consciousness. By then, his combat experiences had triggered automatic, perhaps instinctive, responses that were devoid of anything like a "feeling". If and when he survived a battle, then he might think about how it had all unfolded – but probably not. Most importantly, visible or invisible, he overrode any terror or hesitancy.

Again, Saburo and Kitaro survived, though not totally unscratched. The left side of Kitaro's face was badly cut by a few bits of shrapnel from a German grenade. He was lucky that they did not get his eye. After he was patched up by the medic, he and Saburo joked about whether the inevitable scar would detract or improve his sex appeal.

"I guess, I did not stick close enough to you," Kitaro laughed.

"I am not sure flying metal has eyes or intention to select its targets," Saburo quipped. "Invisibility works best when someone is trying to see you well enough to shoot you."

"Well, then, maybe the salvation spell that envelopes you – still works," Kitaro smiled.

"It did this time," Saburo commented while he mentally began to assess the odds and probabilities that he would continue to be so lucky.

But lucky they were. They continued to skirmish with the Germans until they passed the town of Sasseta. A couple of days of rest and again, on July 1st they were thrown into the breach along the Arno River and a savage struggle for Hill 140 and Castellina Marittima. Over the next 25 days or so they slugged German positions and suffered about 1,100 killed or wounded while taking 40 miles of ground.

Finally, Saburo suffered his first injury in one of the firefights. It was nothing worthy of a Purple Heart, which was being won left and right by hundreds of his comrades. As he was advancing with a patrol, a German machinegun opened up, and instinctively he flung himself flat to the ground. In the process, though, he broke his fall with his left arm and badly sprained his left wrist. He barely noticed the pain at first, but when he went to level his rifle, he noticed his left hand was not operating quite right. He fought on with just his right arm doubting if his shots were very accurate.

While they rested a bit in the middle of September near Naples, Saburo noticed the effects of nerves seeping into the psyches of many of the survivors in his Company. Increasingly their eyes were clouding up and at times their hands would begin to tremble. Often, they would begin to jabber in a rapid cadence about anything or everything as if to expel some contagion in their souls. Those who like Saburo and Kitaro remained relatively calm and normal stood out and the NCOs and officers tried their best to "buddy" them up with the newbies who were filtering into the unit as replacements. Saburo accepted the responsibility but worried if he would be able to preserve his charge when the time came.

28

"Oh god," Saburo lamented. "Another hill to capture!"

"Yeah, man, it seems like all we do is fight uphill," Kitaro shrugged. "Just once, I'd like to be on top and have those Krauts come up at us."

They had been jousting with the Germans since the middle of October as they were maneuvered into the Rhone Valley and positioned to take four hills in the Vosges Mountains the Germans held controlling the town of Bruyeres. The terrain was very different than what they had been used to in Italy. The hills were irregular and steep in some places and the forest thick and foggy in the days and pitch-black dark at night. For five days the 100th Battalion of the 442nd fought seesaw battles with the Germans for those four hills. The struggle shrunk the fighting strength of the 100th by over a hundred men. Saburo and Kitaro were still upright and able to fight though they were getting so weary they could barely stand.

"Look at that place, swarming with Germans," Saburo observed from the heights overlooking Biffontaine. Dropping his pack and plopping himself down, Kitaro lit up a cigarette, and nodding his head towards the town below he said with relief, "Glad we don't have to dislodge those Krauts. Let some other 442nd guys do it. We've earned a rest taking these hills."

Then early the next morning they were jostled out of their snug foxholes when Sergeant Kohashi shouted, "Saddle up men, we're on the move."

"Oh, gosh Sarge, can't we just stay here a little bit longer and watch the Germans get chased out of the town. We are in such a good position – a regular bird's eye view." Kitaro pleaded.

"Come on private, who do you think is going to eliminate those Germans?" the Sergeant said as he continued to roust the men to activity.

"Oh shit!" Saburo nearly shouted. "You mean we're going to do it?"

"Well, Mrs. Roosevelt isn't here to do it, so I guess we'll just have to,"

"Aren't there some other units who need unit citations and to bump up their purple heart average?" Saburo whined.

"Look soldier, ours is not to reason why but ours is to …."

At that point half a dozen other fellows chimed in simultaneously "do and die."

"That's what I am afraid of, Sarge. You realize, of course, that recent statistics prove that the death rate in this unit is one per person." Kitaro said with a touch of black humor.

Carefully descending from the hills, they had bled red for, they entered the town and engaged its defenders in house to house fighting for two days. Though some firefights were intense, an increasing number of Germans soldiers sought the mutual life-saving approach by surrendering. In the two weeks that the 100th had engaged the Germans, they had captured an odd assortment of prisoners.

Saburo arrived at a holding pen with what he referred to as "volunteers for peace". "Hell, the German army must be getting desperate," Saburo said waving to the rag-tag lot of prisoners in the pen. "There are Poles and Yugoslavs over there," pointing to one corner of the pen. "And over there it seems like there are a couple of Somalis and even three East Indians from something called the Freies Indien Regiment. Where the hell is Somaliland anyway?"

"Don't know," one fellow called out. "Maybe somewhere near India?"

"Yeah, it's weird," said the sergeant taking custody of the prisoners. "Many of them don't speak much German and who the hell around here speaks Somali?"

"I don't imagine they will be able to organize an escape," quipped one of the MP guards.

"I don't think they will want to. Did you see what their field rations were? At least now they can have some hot meals, coffee, and cigarettes."

"Right," said another guard. "Maybe that's why they surrendered in the first place."

As the dust settled on Bellefontaine, the ambulatory members of the 100th threw themselves into "resting" with abandon. They were promised a long rest, but experience had taught them that that could be changed at the drop of a hat. And much to their chagrin two days later they were reassembled and sent into battle.

General John E. Dahlquist sent them up the steep incline of the thick pine forest ahead of them. They were not told the true nature of their mission, just to take the top of the hill. They moved out at 3:00 am on October 27th into thick fog, rain and snow that made the going slippery and muddy. Visibility was so poor they had to hold on to the pack of the man in front of them so they would not get separated or lost.

"You go first," Kitaro said to Saburo. "After all you are invisible."

"But if I go first and I am invisible, doesn't that mean that they will see you," Saburo said half-joking.

"Ok, then we'll flip for it," Kitaro said retrieving an Italian coin from his pocket that he was keeping for good luck.

Saburo called heads and tails it was.

"Ah what the hell," Kitaro said. "I'll take the lead for a while then when the shooting starts, we can switch."

It was not long before the shooting started, and they both fell off to either side to take cover. The difficult terrain combined with artillery and at times withering fire stalled their progress. The whole company barely inched its way forward having to pause as they encountered mines and other bobby traps. It was difficult to know how effective or ineffective their return fire was. After the first whole day, they had managed to crawl barely 30 yards up the slope.

Saburo and Kitaro dug in after the first day as deeply as they could. They caught only cat naps for everyone was afraid of possible German counterattacks. They could hear sounds like the Germans were moving around in the dark and concluded that they were probably repositioning themselves for the inevitable renewal of the onslaught the next morning.

Sure enough, around 5:00 am, the NCOs passed around and got everyone ready for another push. Having wolfed down parts of the C-Rations he carried, Saburo felt uneasy about the whole mission. They were literally stabbing in the dark and equally in dark as to why. Fewer troops began the crawl than the day before. It did seem, though, that the fire was a little less intense. Maybe the German ranks were thinning as well.

After two more days of basically the same, their Lieutenant finally circulated around and told them what they were trying to do. It seems that some 275 members of the 'Alamo Regiment' of the Texas National Guard had advanced too far and fast into the German defenses and gotten surrounded when their flanks collapsed. They were besieged, running out of water, food, and medical supplies, and threatened with annihilation. Earlier rescue attempts for the "Lost Battalion" had failed but had enveloped a few German positions in the process. Each side fought to rescue their men and eliminate their enemies and the 442nd was assigned the task of relieving the "T-patchers."

Upon hearing the explanation, Saburo could only remember all the times he and Eiji had played the rescuing cavalry in their childhood heroic imaginations. The fact that they were trying to save Texans seemed to be ironically right to Saburo. He strapped on his web belt complete with a couple of grandees, extra ammunition, and a field bandage, and turned to Kitaro.

"C'mon partner," in an affected Texas accent. "Let's go rescue that wagon train of T-patchers. I'll take the lead today." As they set out Kitaro heard Saburo starting to say something he did not understand. He thought it might have been Chinese.

"Beitan shidai tongzhi Zhe
Baohu women cong
Womende weilai" Saburo softly whispered.

"What's that?" Kitaro asked.

"Oh, something I learned from my best friend Eiji's father – Morio. "It is a little prayer to be protected from whatever misfortune that might be lurking in the hours and days before us."

"Think it will work?" Kitaro asked.

Saburo turned around and smiled at Kitaro. Pounding his chest and right arm with his free left hand he boasted, "You don't think I have been 'invisible' by accident, do you?"

They had finally crept far enough that they could see the edge of the hillcrest behind the German bunkers. The heroism of their buddies continued to manifest itself.

Faced with insurmountable obstacles and hopelessly pinned down, the only remaining officer of the advance company, recklessly stood up, beckoned to his sergeant to follow him, and commenced to charge the Germans. The rest of the company witnessed that and one by one they rose up and charged as well. They all began shouting "Banzai! Banzai!" Off to their right, they saw one fellow get shot in the head. For sure he was dead. But then a couple of minutes, bleeding profusely, he popped up, grabbed his helmet, and continued to advance up the hill.

Saburo and Kitaro joined the insane rush towards the summit. Just then Saburo's right elbow and arm seemed to explode. It almost felt like his arm was being ripped from his shoulder socket. Strangely, though, there was a momentary time lag between when the bullet hit his elbow and he began to experience any pain. Saburo slumped down and looked at his right arm basically dangling by just a few threads of skin, muscle, and tendons. "Shit," he said as he realized that his arm was basically useless.

"Saburo!" Kitaro called out. "Saburo!" He began to move towards his downed partner.

Saburo was fumbling with his left hand buttoning his right shirt button to one of the buttonholes of his shirt to make a crude sling. "Stay where you are, Kitaro. I think I can handle this," grimacing in pain. He then fumbled to get his field bandage out and tried his best to wrap it around his bleeding elbow.

Kitaro arrived and began to help staunch the bleeding and secure the bandage. "I'll go get a medic if we have any left," he announced and started down the hill a bit. He turned around to check on Saburo before leaving and it was then that the bullet ripped into his chest. He let out a confused and shocked "Ooff" and doubled over clutching his torso near his heart. He fell on his back and began staring straight up to the top of the pine canopy and the faint glimmer of light in the sky.

Saburo tried to get to him, but the bullets were hitting all around him. He could hear Kitaro making a hissing noise and he realized that he had a sucking chest wound. He had to get to him and help him. Fumbling with his left hand, Saburo got a package of cigarettes and removed the cellophane outer cover. As he crawled to Kitaro, he was going to try to put it over the hole in his chest to stop the sucking.

It seemed to take forever to get to him. When he got there, Saburo reached out, ripped away Kitaro's shirt with his left hand and teeth, and began to put the cigarette cover over the bubbling, gurgling hole in his chest. He raised up just a little to call out for help from someone below. Just then a bullet ripped into the right side of his back knocking the wind out of him and laying him flat on his face. Then everything went black.

29

"Looks like you're going home, soldier," a voice from the end of his cot penetrated Saburo's unconsciousness.

Saburo struggled a bit amidst piercing pain to lift his head up to see the speaker. A medical orderly was circling his cot and straightening out his blanket. A bit dazed and groggy Saburo unsteadily moved his left hand over to his right side and began to feel his arm from the shoulder downwards. He did not get very far when he realized that he was just feeling the end of bandages and no more.

"My arm, where's my arm?" Saburo called out.

"We had to take it off. The damage was too bad. That wound in the back was a bigger concern at first. Luckily it only nicked the bottom of your right lung. The surgeons had a bit of a time patching you up," said the medical orderly in what was obviously some field hospital.

Saburo tried to sit up and then realized how painful his torso was and took inventory of those bandages as well. He was short of breath and terribly thirsty. He reached for a glass of water on a box next to the cot and the orderly swiftly swung in and took it first.

"Here, let me help you with that," he said as he lifted the glass of water up to Saburo's lips. He fished out a bottle of pills from his breast pocket and handed two to Saburo. "Better take these with that sip. It might help fight back the pain a bit."

"Kitaro? What about Kitaro?"

"I don't know about any Kitaro, pal. I don't think there is anyone named that here. There's another medical station across the way. I can check there for you if you like? You guys really got mauled but you broke through and saved those Texans. Boy were they happy to see you guy!"

"How long have I been here," Saburo asked.

"Going on three days now. You hungry? Can I get you anything?"

"Just find Kitaro Kasuge for me if you can. I need to know he's alright."

"Ok, pal, I'll ask around. In the meantime, don't get too rambunctious. Here's your bathroom for right now," he said placing a bottle to piss in and a bedpan under the cot within easy reach. "I'll be back in a little bit."

Saburo strained his neck to survey his surroundings. He was in a medical aid station for the recovery of the severely wounded. There was quite a bit of activity as medics flowed around the area attending to other casualties. He was amazed at how many cots were occupied. He recognized a dozen or so of his cot mates and tried to call out to them to see if they knew anything about Kitaro. But he just did not have the wind in him to make himself heard above the moans and sounds of the suffering. Feeling groggy and weary, he slipped back into a shallow slumber.

It was not too long before he felt someone gently rolling him over onto his stomach. With bleary eyes he looked up to see a couple of medics and an officer, no doubt a doctor, carefully unwrapping his bandages to examine his back wound.

"Ah, that's coming along alright," the doctor said. "How you doing soldier?" he asked.

"I hurt from my hips up," Saburo reported.

"That's understandable. But the surgery seems to have gone well enough and now you just have to let your body heal itself."

"What about my arm?" Saburo said doing his best to lift the stump.

"Well, we can't do much about that. You are likely to feel what we call phantom pains where your lower arm and hand once were. They should go away over time. Eventually, you might be able to be fitted for a prosthetic."

"You mean I might get a hook? But I am not a pirate," Saburo said trying to extract a little humor from his situation.

"I suppose you could get a hook if you want. But I think that back in the states somebody will be able to fix you up with something a bit more functional."

Saburo then looked up and saw the medic he awakened to earlier. "Kitaro?"

"He did not make it. I found a Kitaro Kasuge in the morgue. I guess that's your guy," came a softly sad answer.

Hearing Kitaro was dead was like being hit in the chest with a two-by-four. He gasped for air and felt sick to his stomach.

"Take it easy, soldier," the doctor said. "It's tough, but you have to concentrate on getting better yourself. I suspect that as soon as it can be arranged, you'll be shipped back to some army hospital in the States to complete your recovery and rehabilitation. The war's over for you pal. You survived."

Knowing the fate of Kitaro and feeling the stump of his right arm, Saburo was not sure about anything. He almost wished he had died, and Kitaro was in some cot getting attended to.

A couple of days later, Saburo heard the rumors. General Dahlquist called for a parade to be held on November 12th to honor the bravery and sacrifice of the 442nd. Saburo had been getting up and walking around, especially to use the latrine as he hated the bedpan and asked if someone could help him get to the location of the parade.

"Hey man, you can't go. You are maybe the walking wounded, but you are still not fit enough to the parade," said one orderly. "Besides, the parade is at the bivouac area. That's about five miles from here. You want someone to drive you there so you can show off your bloody bandages?" he asked in a half-joke.

He knew it was impractical, but he wanted to be there. To show that general that despite being a Nisei, a previously suspect American, he and all the rest of the 100th/442nd were just as loyal as anyone else and their blood was just as red. He may have lost his arm, but he did not lose his pride in being an American.

In the early evening of the 12th, one of his platoon mates showed up at the recovery station. Saburo was glad to see the familiar face and he and four other wounded members of their company gathered around the fellow to get the latest about their victory and the toll of the battle.

"You should have seen the General." Sergeant Abe Hayashi began. "He was looking out at the whole of the 442nd and seemed totally perplexed."

"Yeah," another of the wounded said. "He was surveying the results of using us as cannon fodder. Sending us on that mission without us even knowing what we were supposed to do for the first couple of days."

Sergeant Hayashi, half smiled and half grimaced as he continued. "I overheard him call out to the Major, 'I thought I told you to assemble the whole unit. I ordered everyone out today! Why are there so few here!' The Major simply replied, 'That's all there is, sir.'"

After a drag on a cigarette, Sergeant Hayashi somberly added, "When Companies I and K marched by there were only eight men in Company I and eighteen in Company K. That's twenty-six left out of the four hundred that started up the hill."

Everyone there gasped and both felt lucky to be alive but pity for the dead.

"When the General saw that, I heard him gasp – "Oh God."

30

"Oh, my God, he's been hurt" gasped Yua Jahana as she looked down at the official telegram from the Army. Sobbing loudly, she looked up. "He's been wounded, Yo! Good heavens, what are we going to do?"

Yo took the telegram gently from her hands and began to read it so intently that he almost burned a hole in its fragile flypaper.

"But he's alive, Yua, he's alive!" Yo exclaimed with relieved yet nervous excitement. "He's being discharged and coming home."

"Home," Yua shouted angrily. "Home! What home? You call this home?!"

Yo reached out to soothe her and try to calm her down. Yes, the prospect of a wounded Army veteran having loyally served the

156

government being returned to a barbed-wire encampment imprisoning his family seemed almost too much to take. His blood pressure started to climb, and he wanted to scream at the top of his lungs at the injustice of it all. But he held himself in check, focusing on the reality that their son was alive and the hope that they would soon be able to see him regardless of the circumstances. The nature of his wounds, how and when he would be back in the country, and where he might end up were all painfully missing from the brief telegram. Yua began to thrash around the barracks and throw things on the floor. "Are they going to send him back here?"

"We don't know. But if they do, we'll make the best of it, Yua. At least we'll be able to take care of him. Aimi is a nurse, and I am sure she'll help out with whatever we might need to help him heal."

Their minds began to spin and swirl with all the harsh realities that they were facing. The camp had begun to fracture and disintegrate because of the draft resisters and the growing anti-government sentiment. On July 1, 1944, Congress had passed the Renunciation Act allowing the Nisei and Kibei to renounce their American citizenship. Several dozen of the Heart Mountain recalcitrants had already done so. Gaku Nakamura was an Issei, so he had no American citizenship to denounce. But his vociferous and boisterous objections to internment and the policies of the government were noted and his voice spoke for his wife, also an Issei, and helpless Nomo who was a citizen by birth.

Initially, only Gaku was pulled out and sent to Tule Lake where the "disloyals" were being collected and isolated from the rest of the camps. Cho and Nomo faced difficult decisions and eventually, Cho decided to take Nomo with her and opted to accept a transfer to Tule Lake. Under pressure from her father, Nomo, tortured by conflicting allegiances, and a minor child, had her citizenship renounced by her father for her. As a result, the whole family was put on the list of rejected residents and citizens who were going to be repatriated back to Japan regardless of the results of the war.

Aimi had pleaded with Nomo to refuse to go to Tule Lake and even gotten her father and mother to agree to "adopt" her to keep her at Heart Mountain. But Nomo just could not untether herself from her parents. Aimi was deeply depressed when Chu and Nomo departed. At their last meeting, Nomo tearfully handed Aimi her Girl Scout uniform of which she was so proud. She knew her father would explode if he saw it when they reunited. With a gentle and respectful gesture, Aimi accepted it and promised to preserve it for some better, hoped-for future, the doubt and uncertainty of which rubbed their emotions raw. That was a month ago and Aimi was struggling to rebound from the departure of her young charge and friend.

Cho entered the Takara barracks empty of the Nakamuras and with a pained look on her face handed Aimi the telegram. Aimi took it and started to read it. She scanned it intently for any medical information or news that might suggest to her the nature of Saburo's injuries. But there was none. It was just a short telegram stating he was wounded and announcing he would be returned to the United States.

Relieved that he was alive but punched by the possible gravity of his condition, Aimi's woefulness welled up to swell the swamp of her emotions. She began to consider if and what she would tell Eiji in her next letter. She thought it best to wait a bit until they knew more of Saburo's status and condition. Maybe there would be good and optimistic news to send off to Eiji still uniformly doing his part to end the war.

About a week later they received a letter from Saburo himself. It was typed, which was unusual for him and the first clue as to the nature of his wounds. He mentioned that an orderly was typing the letter for him since his wounds included the amputation of his right arm just above his elbow. Since he was right-handed, he had not yet mastered the art of writing with his left hand, but he assured them he was making progress. He was a bit vague about his wound in the back. All in all, he seemed upbeat and urged everyone not to worry. He was getting the best care the Army could provide and he certainly appreciated the improvement in his diet. He was not exactly sure when it would happen, but he told them that he was going to be sent to Bushnell General Military Hospital in Brigham City, Utah. He hoped that he could recover there sufficiently to go and visit them in a couple of months. Finally, he suggested that they could tell Eiji that he had won enough purple hearts for the both of them.

Time for everyone at Heart Mountain seemed to drag as 1944 began to tick its way to the end of the year. Everyone was agitated and anxious for their thousand-day ordeal to end. The news of the war was such that in Europe and Asia, America's enemies were cornered and back on their hind legs. Whatever imagined necessity for the relocation and America's concentration camps was long since passed. Finally, long overdue in the minds of the prisoners of faces looking like the enemy, FDR announced in December that Japanese Americans might begin to return to the West Coast if they could. That begged the question of a return to what. Still, the announcement was welcomed and the remainder of the residents of Heart Mountain went into a buzz of activity and anticipation of their release and returned freedom.

Throughout their incarceration, the Takaras and Jahanas had been terribly strapped by the loss of their incomes. The promised revenues from Eiji's land near Oxnard had dried up. Morio and Yo had consistently volunteered for any and all jobs in the camp and the surrounding countryside to earn whatever they could. Eiji and Saburo had sent as much of their Army pay home as they possibly could. Together they decided that to make a go of it back at their old home --the Takara homestead. They would combine their resources and keep up the mortgage payments on that house. Sad though they were, they reassured themselves that if and when they were able to return to Santa Monica, they could lodge together until they could get back on their feet financially. At least they had a target to aim for and, depending on conditions, a roof over everyone's head. That also relieved some of the stress about what to do with Saburo. With a little luck, the timing of all the parts in motion might allow them to reunite with Saburo in California.

The Takaras and Jahanas were among the first families to get in line to return to California in January 1945 as the egress from Heart Mountain was being organized.   They each were given $25.00 and a one-way ticket to Los Angeles. They packed up only what they thought they would need to get reestablished in Santa Monica and distributed among friends some of the camp survival implements they had fashioned and accumulated over the two-and-a-half years they had been there. Without even a hint of nostalgia, with spirits soaring yet tamped down by fears of what they might find at their destination, they boarded the train to go "home".

31

"Oh my god!" uncontrollably escaped Eiji's mouth as he completed translating an accidentally intercepted mayday message from a Japanese transport ship. "Jesus, what the hell was he thinking?" Eiji continued to yell at his desk, nobody in particular, and to the air around him. "Damned submarine commander out to bag any Japanese ship he can hit." Normally such a message would be a navy affair, but the ship's captain put it out on multiple emergency channels desperately seeking help.

"What's up, Eiji?" Sergeant Williams asked, as he quickly moved to Eiji's desk. He noticed Eiji was doing his best to hold back tears.

"It's a distress call from a freighter sailing from Okinawa," Eiji said.

"Ship hit by torpedoes. Women and 700 children aboard. Few lifeboats. Sinking fast. Help! Anyone in the area help!" was the translation Eiji's trembling hand to Sergeant Williams. The Sergeant noticed that Eiji was fighting back tears.

"Tough break soldier, but given the enormity of this war, this is small potatoes, sad though it might be."

But to Eiji, the officers wearing the uniform of the United States bore a responsibility to be as diligent as possible in where they threw their ordinance. Like millions of other innocents over the decade, those passengers on that ship did not deserve their watery graves.

Eiji and nearly the whole intelligence assessment resources of the army and navy combined had detected that the Imperial General Headquarters had issued a revised doctrine sometime in the middle of August 1944 entitled "Essentials of Island Defense". The newer strategy was to abandon attempts at defending against amphibious invasions at the water's edge and instead ordered inland defenses anchored on fortifications, mobile and concealed forces, and above all, last stand fighting to the death. Acknowledging that, it was learned that as early as June 1944 the Japanese war ministry and cabinet approved the evacuation of civilians from Okinawa. Neither Eiji nor anyone else could know if that was for humanitarian or strategic reasons clearing the decks, so to speak, to allow the Army defending the island greater freedom of movement unimpeded by civilians.

Over the next weeks, Eiji did his best to secretly garner information about Okinawa as it was clearly in the gunsights of allied forces. The sinking of the transport ship seemed to suspend evacuations from the island. But they began to pick up again and Eiji suspected that the influential authorities on the island had succeeded in convincing some of the populous to risk leaving. Eiji did whatever he could to check on ship sinkings and sub attacks and perhaps the navy took notice of its mistake in August as no others happened.

Meanwhile, the new island defense strategy seemed to account for the relatively uncontested landing MacArthur made in the Philippines at Leyte in October 1944. Eiji buckled down and worked as hard as he could handling the dozens of intercepted messages, fewer and fewer of them bothered much with being coded and matching that information with the intelligence gathered by some of his classmates and fellow alumnae of the MIS training who were debriefing Japanese prisoners of war. Still, he could not take his mind off of Okinawa and wished he could be more directly involved in that operation.

"I am telling you again, corporal Takara, you are staying with us and that's it," said Sergeant Williams as he entered the area where Eiji and a few other translators and intelligence men did their work. The Sergeant knew what Eiji would ask as soon as the sergeant arrived, so he headed off the inquiry.

"You are too valuable to release to those Navy guys, so you are stuck with us. Why do you want to jump ship, so to speak, now anyway.?"

Eiji knew it was a long shot, but he could see the direction the offensives against the Imperial Japanese Army and Navy was going. MacArthur was hell-bent on keeping his promise of "returning" to the Philippines and liberating them. That was all well and good, though Eiji suspected there was a good dose of arrogant ego involved in the general's determination. But Eiji could also see that Admiral Nimitz's forces were approaching Japan from the southeast and were likely to be island hopping right to Japan's doorstep.

"I'm tired of army food, sarge," Eiji said while cracking the hint of a smile.

"You think the Navy has better food?" the sergeant protested. "Even if they do, you are likely to blow it all over if you are on some ship that gets rained on by the Japanese."

The sergeant walked around and examined the work that Eiji and the others were doing. "Besides, corporal Takara, we are all going to move soon anyway. We need to keep up with the general. The landing at Leyte was such a cakewalk that the general personally and ostentatiously waded ashore. He wants us to move up with him to Tacloban."

"Where, Sarge?" another voice called out.

"It's a city on the coast of Leyte. We'll be closer to the general's operations but lately, he has shown a preference for commanding from the bridges of light cruisers."

Eiji grabbed one of the maps they had strewn about the room. He located the place and judged that it was still about 1,000 miles from Okinawa, which was increasingly on Eiji's mind. The scuttlebut and the strategic logic suggested that there would be a major push to capture Okinawa soon and that the Navy would probably be in the driver's seat for that campaign. Eiji had only felt a whisper of violent vengeance over his participation in the elimination of Admiral Yamamoto and virtually no wrath for all those dispatched at the Marianas Turkey Shoot. But as the climate and landscape increasingly reminded him of his days at "Some Place Else," he was getting more and more worried about whether providence might preserve or pummel his beloved relatives and friends.

"I hope Grandfather Ono, Kineshiro san, Mirai, who should be about five years old by now, and all the others have gotten out. All you "Some Place Elsians," please go someplace else." Eiji thought and sometimes whispered to himself.

32

"Look, we decided not to leave," Kineshiro san, dressed neatly in the uniform of an air raid warden, reminded his compound mates as they assembled to review their plans and strategies. He was by no means committed to the Japanese military or their war. Because of his age, he was not drafted into the auxiliary forces as many of the younger men on the Island had been. Still, he accepted the role of an air raid warden and wore the uniform smartly if only to deflect suspicion and doubts about his real feelings.

"The chance that those ships might get torpedoed was too great," he continued. "And relocating the elderly and children to the barren north of the island as ordered by the army would only be a recipe for different disasters."

Kineshiro san reflected for a bit on how he was glad that Grandfather Ono had died peacefully, just a year before. The pressures of the war had increasingly squeezed all of Japan like some giant boa constrictor, and especially Okinawans, since the nation went on full war mobilization in 1943. Grandfather Ono was spared any further deprivations and was safely in eternity.

"You all know that General Cho admitted in January the army's intention to confiscate all food should the island be invaded to alleviate any duties to the civilians that might degrade the army's fighting abilities. "Kineshiro san continued, taking Mirai's little hand into his. "We must be ready to be self-sufficient and protect ourselves. We have food stockpiled and hidden around here. We can seek refuge in the caves near the Seifa Utaki shrine. With any luck, Amamikyu will protect us."

There was a murmur in the group between and among the men who had been conscripted by the army into the self-defense "volunteer" force.

"I know you guys have been drafted into the auxiliary forces of the Imperial Japanese Army, or whatever. I see Deputy Sato coming here every day to gather you up for training and practice. But you have to decide where your loyalties really rest."

The younger men were shifting about and looking down at their feet.

"The Japanese came here decades ago and completely swamped and displaced us Okinawans. You all know why we call this little community "Some Place Else". Are you going to defend and protect the Japanese oppressor who looks down on you as some sort of incomplete human? Or are you going to remain true to us, your family and friends who have fed you, taken care of you, and stood by you all these years?" Kineshiro san appealed. "Are you willing to die for those who would do the same to others as they have done to us Okinawans? Has their propaganda about the nobility of dying for the emperor mesmerized you into seeking some fictitious nobility and glory getting yourselves blown to pieces?"

The crowd was quietly nervous as they listened to Kineshiro san.

"Instead, when the time comes and you get called, go with us to the caves. Use your weapons to defend us from those Japanese army guys who have already raped our women and intend to steal our food. Preserve yourselves and our family for whatever future might spring from the ashes of this war." He concluded dramatically but he could not gauge the effect and result. Only time would tell.

The next morning Captain Sato, who had been absorbed into the reserve Army and took that rank as being superior and more prominent than "Deputy" showed up, as usual, to collect the "volunteers" to go through their paces as defenders of Japan. The food rationing system which had been in place for some time meant that there were no delectable tidbits for him to scarf down as in times before. Either that or the gnawing nervousness of the horizon of hopelessness they all faced put Captain Sato in a generally grumpy mood. As he marched the men off to drill, Kineshiro san watched closely to detect their keenness for the cause. It seemed it was not very high.

A thousand miles away Eiji was met at his office by two Navy intelligence officers wanting to interview him. After introductions, the trio sat down together, and Eiji was debriefed of all he remembered about his days in Okinawa. He suddenly realized the drill; they were trying to generate or confirm targets for bombings and shellings and gather more detailed topographical understandings. Eiji then knew that an invasion was imminent.

"I was last there some five years ago, so some of what I know may be out of date," Eiji began. "But it is likely that they will use Shuri Castle between Naha and Nishihara as an anchor for their defenses," Eiji said knowing that a fight there would be perilously close to "Some Place Else." He sketched out as much of the terrain as he could remember. But knowing how Okinawans felt about the Seifa Utaki shrine and its significance to the residents of "Some Place Else," he was conflicted and did what he could to minimize the military significance of the location. Given his known intimacy of the island, he requested that he be loaned to the strike forces to do what he could to mitigate the misery and convince Okinawans to surrender.

Two days later, Sergeant Williams bellowed through the hallway at Eiji. "Corporal Takara, grab you your go bag and get ready to fly out of here,"

"What?" Eiji asked as he was caught off guard.

"You are going to do actual fieldwork."

"What does that mean?" Eiji asked.

"You are being reassigned to the 77th Infantry Division in the special Tenth Army scheduled to capture and secure Okinawa."

Eiji was gobsmacked. He could not believe his luck. Not only was he going to get nearer to the operation, but he would be actually in it, on the ground, and may be able to do his best to mitigate some of the brutality of the battle.

"Get your gear together chop, chop," Sergeant Williams said. "You are supposed to fly to the staging area with the Navy guys at 17:00."

A squall of sensations surged through Eiji as he rushed to his billets to collect what he wanted to take with him. He was hopeful that he could survive the typhoon of steel that was about to rain down on the island. Being close to the action, he was aware that there would be some danger involved. Reports he read from the assault on Iwo Jima reaffirmed the Japanese command's orders to fight to the death were followed to devastating effect all around including the civilian population.   He knew he would be reoutfitted when he got to the 77th so he only grabbed a few things, a few mementos from his days in Australia, a few pictures of Aimi and Nomo and the family, the letters from Aimi and Saburo. For certain he carefully packed his cowboy hat.

33

Aimi was doing her best to minimize all the fussing that ensued as the Takaras and Jahanas detrained at Union Station in Los Angeles. The group of them paused on the platform for a few minutes and took deep breaths as the train disgorged slightly over a hundred returning Issei and Nisei from Heart Mountain. Having spent more than two days on the train, they were wrinkled and worn out. It had been over two years since they were in Los Angeles and while they were almost overjoyed to have returned, they were also filled with apprehension about what they might find when they got back to their "home". The ugly claws and teeth of racism had come out back in 1941 and they worried that they were still poised to make their lives miserable upon their return. FDR in his first press conference after his re-election in November 1944 had proposed the idea that it would be better for the Japanese Americans and the country as a whole if they were scattered around the country rather than reconcentrating themselves on the West Coast. He affirmed that they were American citizens and publicly praised the heroism and sacrifice of the Nisei soldiers on the battlefields of Italy.

The President's preferences did not dissuade their little group from attempting to recover the only life they had known in America which was in the greater Los Angeles area. Besides, they looked forward to their reunion with Saburo as he was released from Bushnell General Military Hospital in Utah and his train was scheduled to pull into the station late that afternoon. Because of that, the group split up. Morio, Kiku, and Aimi agreed to go directly to their house and to see if they could start getting it suitable for habitation by everyone. Yo and Yua were going to hang around the station and collect Saburo and then join them later.

Preserving their limited capital, they dragged their luggage to the bus stop to get to Santa Monica. When the first bus opened its doors and saw them waiting to board, the bus driver just closed the doors and pulled away. Then they were joined by a Nisei soldier wearing his paratrooper uniform complete with campaign medals. When the next bus door opened, he stepped aside to let the Takaras board. Just then a woman behind them in line yelled out to the bus driver, "Damn Japs. Don't let them get on the bus!" The bus driver saw the fellow in uniform and said, "I don't know lady, looks like here is an American soldier and maybe his family. I think you ought to apologize to them."

As they rode to the stop nearest their home, they looked out the window and saw signs saying still spewing hate. "No Japs wanted here." "We don't cut Jap hair." "Send all the Japs back." Descending from the bus they hobbled their way up the hill towards their house. When they got there their breath was pulled out of their lungs by what they saw. The house was covered with hateful graffiti in red paint. The formerly well-manicured yard was mostly dead from lack of care. The windows were boarded up and shards of broken glass lay beneath them. They had obviously been smashed but someone had come and "fixed" them with -plywood sheets. Morio wondered how and who.

When they pushed past the cobwebs at the door and entered the house a stale and dusty air greeted them. The interior had not been disturbed as best as they could tell. It had become the denizen of spiders and bugs of various sorts and certainly needed a thorough cleaning. Kiku went to the kitchen and tried to turn the water on only to hear the pipes shudder with a low gurgling sound and mostly air. Aimi flipped a light switch, and nothing happened.

"We'll have to have the water and electricity turned on tomorrow," Morio said.

Kiku threw out, in a brave and nearly cheery voice, "Well, Aimi, looks like its candles tonight and sandwiches from the deli. Let's find some rags and start trying to clean up a bit."

"I am going over to the Andrew's place to see if Clark is home and to see what's up over there," Morio said heading for the door. Across and up the street a little was the home of the only real Anglo friend the Takara's had made in the neighborhood. Clark Andrews had been a merchant seaman for years plying between the United States and Japan. In the process, he had become a bit of a Japanophile and loved things Japanese. In 1939 he returned to dry land taking up a position at the Santa Monica Yacht Harbor in the cleanup resulting from Attorney General Earl Warren's efforts to shut down mobster Tony Cornero's offshore illegal gambling racket based out of the harbor. The "Battle of Santa Monica Bay" had run for three days as government agents had been trying to board Cornero's flagship, the Rex. Clark had met Morio and Kiku as he frequented their fruit stand at lunchtime to get some of Kiku's delicious homemade taiyaki cakes. They struck up conversations and when they realized they lived near each other – they became fast friends.

Morio walked up the sidewalk to the Andrew's front door. Before he could get to it and knock, it swung open, and Clark came out to greet Morio.

Sheepishly and looking a little guilty Clark began, "I got your telegram. Welcome back."

"It is good to be back, I think."

171

"Come in, do you want some tea or something to eat?"

"No, the women are cleaning up a bit, and then we'll get something at the Deli."

"You don't have to do that; we'll fix something here. Got a fully functioning kitchen and an icebox full of food."

"Thanks, Clark, that sounds good. I'll tell the women when I get back."

"I did what I could to protect your house. But some hooligans got to it when I was at work," Clark apologized.

"That's alright. It's just paint. The place needed a new coat of paint anyway." Morio said to alleviate Clark's uneasiness.

"I suppose you want to know about your other stuff," Clark asked.

"That'll be nice."

"Well, let's go and see," Clark said as he led Morio through the house and out the back door.

They walked to a locked wooden garage on the back of the property. Clark fumbled a few minutes for a key on his key ring he obviously used rarely. He unlocked the padlock, and they swung open the garage door. There was Morio's truck, dusty and dirty, but intact. Morio smiled as he approached it and patted it like it was a pet or friend. Then he looked in the bed of the truck. There were a number of boxes, also dirty and dusty but otherwise undisturbed. They housed dishes, household goods, a record player and records, and the family heirlooms they had refused to let the scavengers and bargain hunters sweep up in the frenetic days before their evacuation. He turned to Clark and warmly clasped his hand with both of his.

"Thanks so much, Clark. I can't tell you how much I appreciate this. You've saved much of our heritage and hearts. How can we ever repay you?"

"Don't mention it you and your family and the Jahanas are great Americans and citizens. I hear Saburo got badly wounded fighting in France."

"He did but he's coming home today, and he and Yu and Yua will be living with us until they can get on their feet. But what can we do for you?" Morio pressed.

"How about some of Kiku's delicious taiyaki cakes?" Clark said with a smile beginning to dominate his face.

"You got it, pal – a lifetime's supply!" Morio said with grateful gusto. "A lifetime's supply."

34

The invasion of Okinawa was the largest amphibious operation of the entire war. The 77th Infantry Division began by assaulting the Kerma Islands off Okinawa's West Coast. Eiji was a translator and general intelligence gatherer assigned to the 17th Infantry Regiment. The assault on the Kerma Islands was heavily one-sided with only 20 or so Americans killed and 80 or so wounded compared to an estimated 650 Japanese casualties. There were no captured prisoners for Eiji to debrief or interrogate. But he did have to exert all his energies to dissuade the women on the islands from attacking the GIs with spears. For the most part, he succeeded but he felt terrible each time some woman was cut down charging some American soldier.

From there, in the middle of April, Eiji participated in the attack on Ie Shima Island where the fighting was considerably fiercer. In the first few days when it seemed that resistance had ceased, Eiji was in the chow line when he heard a voice behind him.

"Hey soldier, I want to talk to you," said a voice.

Eiji turned around and saw a 40ish old man in disheveled army fatigues with no unit patches or rank designations walking towards him. The man extended his hand for a handshake and introduced himself.

"I'm Ernie Pyle."

Eiji self-consciously shook his hand. He had heard that the famous correspondent was in their unit to cover the action but never guessed he would meet him.

"What can I do for you Mr. Pyle?" Eiji asked.

"I just want to talk to you about your experiences. Your Japanese American, right?"

"Yes. Born and raised in Santa Monica, California," Eiji said with a touch of pride.

"That's interesting. I think readers would like to hear about Japanese Americans loyally and bravely serving the nation in this horrific mess of slaughter."

"I don't have much of a story, Mr. Pyle."

"Oh, sure you do." Pyle insisted. "What have you been doing?"

"I was recruited as a translator in 1942 and have been doing that ever since. This is my first field assignment."

"Interesting," Pyle said taking out a pad and pencil to take notes.

"I've been mostly an assistant and a behind-the-scenes guy," Eiji confessed. "If you want the story of someone who really did something, then you would want to find Harold Fudenna. He's probably still at MacArthur's headquarters." Eiji shuffled towards the servers to get his plate of whatever mess was being served up.

"But that's just it," Pyle continued. "This whole war is dependent on unsung assistance and assistants like yourself."

"Well, I don't know about that," Eiji said. "I just do what I can."

"Look, soldier, I want to get deeper into your story. But right now, I am supposed to accompany Colonel Coolidge to the new command post they are setting up. I'll try to find you tomorrow if circumstances permit, and we can talk further."

Eiji watched Pyle walk away. He had mixed feelings about being the subject of such attention. All the guys in the 77th liked Pyle and thought of him as their buddy. He helped people back home connect with the real human-interest stories of the war. Eiji also had a flash of thought about what he might do after the war. He thought that maybe he would want to become a writer or newspaperman, like Pyle.

The next day, his Sergeant approached him. "Did you hear Takara? That Pyle guy you were talking to yesterday. He got killed." A vapor of dolor descended on nearly everyone in the unit. Eiji and everyone else felt as if they had lost a true friend.

Later during the fight, a sergeant delivered to Eiji a moderately wounded Japanese lieutenant. He was momentarily stunned when he saw Eiji.

"What are you?" the lieutenant asked Eiji.

"I am an American," Eiji responded with his fluent Japanese.

"No, I mean who are your people – are you Japanese?" the lieutenant persisted.

"I am Okinawan," Eiji proudly announced. "But I did go to university in Tokyo for several years."

The lieutenant was perplexed but his eyes lit up when he saw Eiji pull out a pack of cigarettes. Unwilling to ask for one, the officer looked at Eiji suggesting his craving for a smoke.

"You want one?" Eiji asked.

The lieutenant twitched a slight affirmative nod.

Eiji offered him the pack of Lucky Strikes. When the lieutenant took it and started to hand the pack back, Eiji told him to keep the whole pack.

"I can get more. They come in the C rations," Eiji casually commented.

Despite an initial propaganda prudence about cavorting with the enemy and his shuddering shame at not committing suicide rather than getting captured, the Lieutenant gradually became quite chatty. He kept asking Eiji about how and why his Japanese was so good and Eiji did what he could to reassure the lieutenant that he would not be mistreated.

Borrowing a jeep, Eiji began to take the lieutenant to the assembly point of potentially cooperative prisoners. Suddenly the lieutenant shouted, "Stop!"

Eiji compiled and asked, "Why?"

"Minefield," the lieutenant said pointing to the trail they were about to hit.

"What?" Eiji asked. "How do you know?"

"Because I put them there."

They hesitated for a few minutes. Then the lieutenant said, "Give me your bayonet" as he got out of the jeep. Eiji somewhat nervously handed over his blade.

The lieutenant then began to crawl on his stomach in a serpentine pathway forward. Every few feet he paused and carefully poked the ground with the bayonet. Then he would dig a little and carefully extract a land mine. When he was done, he had removed sixteen mines and carefully put them aside. Eiji was amazed. He resolved to get a whole carton of cigarettes for the lieutenant when they got to the rear area.

Everywhere Eiji went he was stared at by both sides. He took to wearing a big American flag sewn on the back of his fatigues to lessen the chance of being shot by GIs. The few Okinawans and rare Japanese he encountered looked at him as if he were some sort of race traitor. A couple of guys in his company took a shine to him and they basically shadowed him wherever he went out of friendship and the "liberation" of some delectable goodies that Eiji could often find in the smoldering ruins of buildings.

After some sharp engagements, Ie Shima Island was secured, and the army had captured another useful Japanese airbase. Pummeled largely to rubble by areal bombings and naval bombardments, Naha was almost completely abandoned as the 77th rolled into the city. The strategies embodied in the "Essentials of Island Defense" played out as the Japanese abandoned the airbases and retreated to set up their defense in the interior. Eiji felt pangs in his stomach as he gazed at places that he had known in different circumstances. Eiji had also correctly predicted that Shuri Castle would be the anchor of the defense of the southern part of the island. Weeks of bitter fighting ensued as the Americans tried to break through and roll up the Shuri defense line. The situation was made all the worse for the numbers, sometimes dozens, even hundreds, of civilians who either attempted human kamikaze attacks on the Americans or opted for mass suicide rather than fall in the hands of their enemies. Eiji was repeatedly frustrated, sometimes to tears, when he failed to convince any ears who could hear him that they had nothing to fear by desisting from their dances with death and surrendering. Sometimes when he used the Okinawan vernacular and dialect he broke through. But his heart continued to get bruised when he did not.

35

"We have to get out of here before Deputy Sato gets here," Kineshiro san shouted reverting to Captain Sato's former role in the community.

Kineshiro san purposely dressed in his air raid warden's uniform surveyed the damage to "Some Place Else". Whether it was an errant bomb or a deliberate attack, the explosion that rocked the place, fortunately, did not kill anyone. But its force did knock down some of the walls to the structures as well as the sign welcoming people to "Some Place Else".

"Ahane, you take your family and the Chinens to cave number two. Make sure you have your allocation of rice and dried fish. You should be able to gather some vegetables to take with you on the way." Kineshiro said in a calm command voice.

"Miyashiro you your group to cave number three. The same applies to you regarding the rice and the fish." Looking at two of the teenage boys who were in the Mayashiro group, Kineshiro san shouted, "What the hell are you doing with these?" He reached to grab the grenades the two had hung from their belts. "Give me those things! You are not taking those into the cave! I know Deputy Sato ordered you to use them against the Americans, but that's just foolish suicide for a lost cause. Now go do something useful and lead the groups through the minefield that you and Deputy Sato planted there the other day."

Turning to the crowd that was scurrying around frantically for survival. "The rest of you come with me and we'll go to cave number one. We have already planned this out. Get into those caves. Hide yourselves and wait for the storm to pass," were Kineshiro san's words as the evacuation of "Some Place Else" commenced.

The ragged troupe began to file out through the rear of the compound and headed up the hill to the designated caves. They passed through the fields that still had some edibles growing and everyone grabbed what they could add to what they were already carrying. They were going to hide out as much from the remaining roving Japanese army units who were likely to press them into being human shields as from the attacking Americans. For over seventy days the battles had raged in the air and on the land around them. The Okinawan population was being served up to the gods as blood sacrifices for the divine emperor in some lunacy hoping to buy time for the next installments of victims to prepare for the inevitable invasion of the home islands. Kineshiro san wondered if the military leaders of Japan actually thought that by inflicting as many casualties on the enemy as possible, the Americans would be so dispirited that that would forestall polluting the sacred soil of Japan with boots on the ground. All he knew was that his responsibility was to preserve as many of the people of "Some Place Else" as possible. The caves seemed to be the best bet.

After Kineshiro san got to cave number one, he and another fellow went into it to inspect it. When they got deep into it, they were taken aback at what they saw. There, in a disheveled and deteriorating old-style Japanese police uniform, were skeletal remains. Kineshiro san did not want to waste too much time inspecting them. A flash of memory was awakened as he pondered if that was the policeman who disappeared those many years ago about the time Morio left for Hawaii. As he heard the sounds of explosions reverberating within the walls of the cave, Kineshiro san looked at the body and said:

> "Beitan shidai tongzhi Zhe
> Baohu women cong
> Womende weilai"

Eiji felt all a tingle as he and the mop-up platoon gingerly approached the compound. For a week he had been revisiting places that he had known so well and was saddened by the destruction before him. Moving out of Nahua they were making their way towards "Some Place Else". So far, the platoon had not been assaulted by either remnant Japanese troops or crazed civilians bent on performing some sort of glorious suicide. They did encounter a couple of lost children whom Eiji was able to soothe somewhat and pass them back to the reception center for detainees. He preferred to think of them like that rather than prisoners because they really were not the enemy.

As they broke through the undergrowth and rounded the corner, Eiji could see the gateway to "Some Place Else". The welcome sign hung half fallen from the archway.

"What's that say?" one of the soldiers asked him.

"Welcome to 'Some Place Else'," Eiji said as he restrained himself from slipping into morose meanders into memories from ten years earlier when things were so different, and everyone's lives were still sprouting positive possibilities. As the men wandered about, Eiji checked on the shed that Deputy Sato had hidden in when he impersonated the Island's governor.

"Doesn't look like anyone's here," the sergeant said. "You know this place corporal Takara?"

"Yeah, I know this place," Eiji almost reluctantly admitted slowly shaking his head in dismay over all that had happened over the years.

"Any idea where the people might have gone?" the sergeant asked.

"Yep, I've got a pretty good idea. Just follow me," Eiji said as he started for the pathway behind the compound."

"Ok men, follow him. Keep your heads on the swivel. Be ready."

The platoon had a few riflemen and one man handling a flamethrower which was being used more and more regularly to flush people out of bunkers and caves. The sergeant constantly kept his Thompson submachinegun at the ready out of a sense of responsibility for the safety of his men. Slowly they filed up the trail led by Eiji. Carrying a rifle himself, though he hoped not to have to use it, he was glad to be in front so the other men would not see his reddening eyes. It was all so sad for him.

Kineshiro san peeked out of the entrance of the cave. There were seven people in there with him including his son, daughter-in-law, and young Mirai. He hoped the other cave groups would be as quiet and careful as he was being. There was no predicting what might happen if they were discovered.

About halfway up the path that Grandfather Ono had taken Eiji on when they went to get water from the well at Seifa Utaki the sergeant called out," Ok, men let' take a little break. Light 'em up if you got 'em."

The men fanned out somewhat on guard but also found places to sit and smoke their cigarettes. Eiji sat down and remembered Grandfather Ono's love of tobacco and the breather they took together at just about the same place. He took off his helmet and ran his fingers through his hair.

"I can't believe it," Kineshiro san whispered as he peeked out of the cave. "It's Eiji!"

"What" murmured quietly the people behind him.

"It's Eiji, I say," Kaneshiro san repeated in amazement.

"What should we do?" his daughter-in-law asked.

"I don't know."

"Should we surrender?" asked his son.

"I'm not sure. Maybe if we do, Eiji can take care of us."

Kineshiro san thought for a minute. Yes, surrendering might be the best and safest thing to do.

"Alright, gather tight behind me," he began. "I'll go out first and get his attention and then you come, alright?"

Kineshiro san turned back to examine Eiji and the disposition of the other soldiers to pick the moment for his egress from the cave.

Eiji realized that he did not have any cigarettes. So, he called out to one of the privates sitting three or four yards to his right.

"You got any butts?"

"Yeh," the young man said reaching into his breast pocket. He got up and started to move towards Eiji who had also risen and was taking a step towards him.

Suddenly they heard a man screaming "Bango! Bango! Bango!" Turning to the sound, they saw Kineshiro san burst from the cave.

With instantaneous reflexes, the man with the flamethrower let loose a blast towards Kineshiro san and the cave's entrance. The sergeant leveled his Thompson and let loose a burst.

Eiji screamed! "No! Stop! Oh god stop!" and rushed towards the immolated man spinning around in a last death throw of pain and flames. Eiji lunged at the man with the flamethrower but not before he let off a second blast at the cave entrance. With exceptional energy, Eiji pulled the device from the soldier crying, "I know that man, I know them. They are my family!"

"What the hell…"

Just then one of the other soldiers rushing towards the point of encounter tripped a mine. The explosion killed its closest victim, wounded two others and the concussion knocked Eiji semi-senseless to the ground. Ears ringing, Eiji refocused his eyes on the blackened chard body before him. He knew it was Kineshiro san. Behind him were the bodies of several others who had either been burned or killed by the sergeant's Thompson. Eiji let out the most soul-wrenching anguished cry anyone has ever heard.

"It was the uniform," protested the soldier as he retook control of the flame thrower. "He yelled charge!"

"He said Bango, not Banzai." Eiji said hanging his head in the palms of his hands. "Bango means no. He was trying to save us from the minefield."

The platoon mates carefully tended to their wounded and dead and Eiji forced himself to examine the bodies of his clan as they were laid out. He knew them all and each death mask pierced his heart as if he was being impaled on stakes. Then he heard a soft whimpering. He looked up and saw Mirai stumbling over the bodies and falling upon her mother's form with her back completely burned off, hugging her and trying to call her back to life. Mirai's hair had been burned off but otherwise, she seemed alright. Probably in those instantaneous increments of eternity, her mother shielded her from the blast.

Eiji stood up and stumbled towards Mirai. He swept her up in his arms and examined her bleeding skull. Cradling her they both began to swim through their tears.

"It was his uniform," the other fellow kept repeating.

"Corporal Takara, get ahold of yourself," the sergeant said. "We did not know who they were. We had only seconds to react." Turning to everyone else, "Be careful men, there are still probably other mines around here."

It was all so undeserved, Eiji thought, so damned undeserved.

36

The Takaras and Jahanas merged together at the Takara house and began to rebuild their lives while waiting for the war to end and Eiji to return. The first order of business was to begin to generate some income. Morio, Yo, and Saburo all went to Oxnard to find out what was going on with Eiji's and Saburo's land. When they got there, they saw the land was under full production and seemed to have been well maintained. That pleased them. But when they tried to locate the man they had entrusted it to, they could not find him. After asking around and doing some digging, they learned that he had quit the area in mid-1943 and gone off to parts unknown. In the process, it seemed that he transferred the caretakership to another fellow – Sam Hopkins. After a couple of hours, they finally located Mr. Hopkins and broached the question regarding the status of the land and how they might get it back.

"Get it back?" Hopkins blurted out at hearing the suggestion. "Get it back? I have no proof that it was ever yours in the first place."

Of course, it was ours. That should have been clearly stated on the deed and land title we left with Mr. Morison," Morio said in a polite but firm voice.

"I don't know any Mr. Morison. I bought this land fair and square from Fred McGrath. We can go to the bank and get the deed and article of transfer from my box at the bank if you want."

"Fred McGrath? We don't know any Fred McGrath." Yo insisted. "This land should be in the name of Eiji Takara and Saburo here," motioning to his son standing to his right.

"Well, it isn't, and I've spent a lot of money improving this place," Hopkins said defiantly.

"We'll take you to court," Saburo declared.

"Go ahead. We'll see how it washes out. According to the letter and spirit of the Alien Land Law of 1924, you Japanese are not supposed to be able to purchase and own land anyway," Hopkins thew back over his shoulder as he began to walk away.

"Maybe so but that's why we put the land in the name of Americans," Morio shouted.

And so, the battle began. Apparently, their "friend" took advantage of the situation and the surging anti-Japanese mania of 1942 and "sold" their land to the McGrath fellow. McGrath then sold it to Hopkins. That explained the cessation of the rent payments and the silence through the years about the situation regarding the land.

They fired up Morio's old but beloved truck which he had retrieved from Clark Andrews and discussed their plans for getting a lawyer and trying to reclaim the land. That would take time and money and generating income was also a topic of intense conversation.

Saburo had already decided to better himself by taking advantage of the benefits he earned through perhaps the single most transformative piece of legislation in the history of the country – the GI Bill of Rights passed by Congress in June 1944. Saburo could receive $500 a year to defray tuition and educational costs. He found out he could go to college at Santa Monica College for about $150 a year. As a single male, he could also get $65 a month living expenses while he was in school. That was not much but living at home would certainly help the whole family with their expenses. So, he enrolled for the summer semester at Santa Monica College.

He was still learning how best to handle his right prosthesis with the two hooks for fingers. He could operate the "hand" by moving his shoulder muscles through the harness he would strap on. He was getting better and better at it with practice. His ultimate goal was to be able to smoke a cigarette with his right "hand" without crushing or dropping it. Though it did not make him whole, he did receive a $95 a month disability from the Veteran's Administration. He put that in the family resource pool once school started, he would be drawing about $160 a month at a time then the average monthly income was about $216.

Morio and Yo were anxious to get some sort of work as well. Antsy to get anything, they approached the Georgian Hotel in Santa Monica and practically begged for work. The manager of the Veranda Restaurant took pity on them and hired them as dishwashers. They were suitably in the back kitchen out of sight but at least they were working. Their wages were dismally low -- $.42 an hour or barely $17 a week. But they were able to start work within a week of their return to the West Coast and that counted for something. Aimi was the luckiest of them all. She was able to resume her career as a nurse at the Japanese Hospital in Boyle Heights earning the princely salary of $170 per month.

Back in the late 1920s Kikuwo Tashiro and four other Japanese physicians pooled their money and founded the Japanese Hospital in Boyle Heights. Initially, the California Secretary of State's office denied them the right to incorporate but they fought the discrimination in the courts and finally won a US Supreme Court decision in the 1927 *Jordan vs. K. Tashiro*. The Japanese community of Los Angeles subscribed to a building fund to the tune of $120,000 and in 1929 the 42-bed Japanese Hospital opened its doors. It prospered until the relocation order of February 1942. Unlike what happened with Eiji's and Saburo's land in Oxnard, Kikuwo was able to lease the hospital to White Memorial Hospital run by the Seventh Day Adventist's Church.

Kikuwo suffered from tuberculosis just before the war and when relocation was enacted he was allowed to stay in Los Angeles for health reasons. But his wife and daughters eventually ended up at the Poston War Relocation camp in Poston, Colorado. Kikuwo used some connections to get his family released from Poston to go work at a farm near Denver where he joined them. Gradually he recovered his health and after the war, they returned to Boyle Heights. By 1946 he had resumed his medical practice and regained the Japanese Hospital from the Seventh Day Adventists. It was there that Aimi resumed her career.

After months of hot and draining work at the Veranda Restaurant Morio and Yo jubilantly left there to work at the largest nursery in Los Angles – the Hashimoto Nursery. Originally founded and operated by the four Hashimoto brothers in 1928 during the war two of the brothers were returned to Japan and another two were interned in the Manzanar War Relocation Camp. After their release at the end of the war, they returned to Los Angles and took up their nursery again. Morio and Yo celebrated their reacquaintance with nature and outdoor work doing what they were best at. Their income was not that much better than at the hotel, but their surroundings were – they worked mostly with other Japanese and enjoyed the feelings of safety in that company.

The Takaras and Jahanas were like thousands of other Japanese and Japanese Americans trying to keep from being drowned in the racial animus they faced and the challenge of being the only immigrant group in the nation's history that had to essentially "make it" twice in their own lifetimes. Starting again from almost zero they had to and did scratch themselves out of their poverty and the undeserved injustices that befell them. Aimi and Saburo in particular gradually began to allow themselves to be optimistic about the future all the while hoping for and anxiously anticipating the safe return of Eiji.

37

Saburo and Aimi were rummaging through all the court records in the Ventura County Courthouse in Ventura. They were searching for a record of the original deed of purchase for the land purchased in in 1931 by Izzy Otani and Eiji. It took some time, but they found it. Then they found the deed that put the land in Eiji's and Saburo's name when Izzy Otani pulled out of the partnership after Eiji returned from Tokyo in 1940. But there was no indication on either deed that Izzy Otani, Eiji Takara or Saburo Jahana were native born US citizens. Both deeds just had their names, which were obviously Japanese, and the address of their abode in Santa Monica. They had left their copies of the deeds with the seemingly good Samaritan Albert Morrison who agreed to work the land and maintain it while the Japanese were relocated and Saburo and Eiji unable to tend the land themselves. Suddenly in April 1942, while the families were in Santa Anita Assembly Center, a deed appeared with Morrison's name on it. Somehow, the land passed from Morrison to a Mr. McGrath and then from McGrath to Hopkins the man who presently claimed he legally owned it. There were records of those transfers taking place in quick succession beginning in June 1942 with Hopkins ending up with the land in October 1942. Nowhere in any of those documents were Saburo or Eiji or any other Japanese names listed.

"It sure looks like some skullduggery was taking place here," Saburo said looking up from the table he and Aimi were seated at and the records they had strewn across it. "Those quick transfers were probably intended to obscure our original ownership."

"That does not change the fact that we have two deeds, one in 1931 and one in 1940 that clearly indicate that Eiji and then you and Eiji were the owners of the land." Aimi protested. "We have a court date coming up. Maybe we ought to get ourselves a lawyer and get ready for it?"

Saburo squinted one eye and pressed his lips together tightly as he thought about that. "We really can't afford a lawyer right now. Besides it ought to be a simple case – there is no record of a legal transfer to Morrison so all rights ought to revert back to us."

Aimi was a bit unsure. "You think we can just go into court and make that case ourselves?"

"Why not? The law is the law, and it is to protect the rights of citizens or at least that is what I always thought." Saburo said with flickering confidence.

With a touch of bitter sarcasm Aimi said, "And you think the events of the last couple of years clearly prove the trustworthiness of the U.S. Constitution and the rule of law?"

"We can only hope," Saburo said. "We can only hope."

When the court was convened, Aimi and Saburo entered the courtroom dressed in their respective uniforms. Aimi looked quite sharp in her pristine white starched and creased nurse's uniform. She wore a bright and shiny American flag lapel pin as an accessory. Saburo was fully decked out in his Army uniform with the two rows of his service medals complete with his Purple Hearts gracing his chest just over his heart. He had even taken the time to polish his mechanical arm in the hopes that it might glisten in some light and further attract the focused attention of the judge. They both took their seats at a table on the left side of the courtroom. They looked over at Mr. Hopkins and his lawyer who seated themselves at the table on the right side of the courtroom. They were dressed in reasonably fashionable business suits also wearing American flag lapel pins.

The judge entered the courtroom. Everybody rose and then sat back down. It all began.

"Alright, lady and gentlemen. I see we have an issue regarding the contested legal ownership of a tract of land on the outskirts of Oxnard, California. Is that right?" the Judge said first reading the documents before him and then looking up at the occupants of both tables.

"Yes, your honor," said everyone almost simultaneously.

"Mr. Freman, good to see you again," the Judge smiled. "I assume you are representing let's see a ...er Mr. Hopkins, is it?"

"That's right your honor," Mr. Freeman said.

Turning to the table with Aimi and Saburo the Judge inquired, "And are you, Seargent Jahana and Ms. Aimi Takara . Are you folks represented by legal counsel?"

Saburo cleared his throat as he was wrestling with the butterflies in his stomach. "No, your honor. I am going to represent our case myself."

The judge cocked one eyebrow in skepticism. "Suit yourself."

The judge took a minute to review the documents both sides had filed. He then looked up and addressed Saburo.

"So, it is your contention that the land in question is rightfully owned by you and a partner, a Eiji Takara, right? Where is he right now?"

"He is still serving in the Army in the Pacific, sir. His sister, Aimi is here to represent his interests."

"I see..." the judge started to rub his mouth with his right hand. "Your claim is based on the 1931 and 1940 deeds of record, right?"

"Yes, sir, they are." Saburo answered.

"Hmmmm," the judge began to ponder.

"And Mr. Hopkins' claim is based on a bill of sale from Mr. McGrath and a 1942 deed, is that right, Mr. Freeman?"

"Yes, your honor, that's right." Mr. Freeman said as Mr. Hopkins nodded his head in agreement.

"And somewhere, here I see a title transfer from a Mr. Morrison to Mr. McGrath, is that right Mr. Freeman?"

"Yes sir."

"So, who are these people Morrison and McGrath?"
Saburo quickly jumped in to answer. "Mr. Morrison was a farmer and landholder of the land abutting our land," he began. "When the orders came for us Japanese to leave the area and assemble for eventual relocation, he approached us and offered to take care of the land for us and give it back to us when we might return."

"I see," the Judge said.

"We gave him the deed and all the paperwork we had regarding ownership so he could take care of taxes and such," Saburo continued.

"That was kind of him, huh," the Judge muttered.

"How the deed and title leapfrogged from Morrison to some McGrath guy and then to Mr. Hopkins here is a mystery to me. It all looks like some sort of fraud or trickery to me" Saburo loudly pointed out.

"Your honor, if I may," Mr. Freeman jumped in.

"Of course, Mr. Freeman."

"The issue here before us is does Mr. Hopkins have a reasonable expectation of legally owning the land.?" Mr. Freeman said, opening his arms up as if to appeal to the Judge's good nature. "To him, he bought the land fair and square. You have the bill of sale there. And for three years now he has worked the land, improved it, and invested his sweat and money into it. Everything all looked legal and above board to my client."

"But it wasn't!" Aimi protested.

Turning towards Aimi, Mr. Freeman asked, "So this Eiji fellow is your brother, right?"

"Yes" Aimi replied a bit cautiously.

"And back in 1931 how old was he when he first became co-owner of the land?"

"He was twelve."

Turning to the judge, "Your honor, I might submit that if any chicanery is the root of this problem, it might be the fact that ordinarily minor children do not purchase land, and this looks like a scheme to get around the California Alien Land Law of 1913 which forbids anyone 'ineligible' for citizenship from owning land."

"But Eiji and I are both citizens," Saburo jumped out of his seat. "Born right here in California, Santa Monica to be precise."

"But there is no..." Mr. Freeman started to continue to make his case.

The judge shuffled through the papers again and put up his hand to silence Mr. Freeman. He took several minutes to think through what might be a reasonable resolution of the problem.

"Ok," the Judge began. "I do not see why Mr. Hopkins should be punished or suffer for having engaged in a business deal that he thought was legitimate and honest."

Mr. Feeman and Hopkins began to nod sensing a victory for their case.

"Yet, clearly there has been some shenanigans that have deprives Seargent Jahana, here, and his partner Mr. Eiji Takara of their land."

Aimi and Saburo began to guardedly become optimistic.

"Sergeant Jahana, I see you've served our country admirably. We are all grateful for your sacrifice. But I am going to award the land to Mr. Hopkins. But Mr. Hopkins, you will pay Mr. Saburo $25 a month for the months you've worked the land up to this month. We'll call it a 'rent-to-purchase' arrangement. That comes to about thirty-four months or about $850 if my math is accurate."

"Eight hundred and fifty dollars!" both Saburo and Mr. Hopkins shouted almost in unison.

"Is worth much more than that," Saburo argued.

"But I already bought the land once and I put plenty of my muscle and money into it since then." Hopkins protested.

"You have just stolen my land," Saburo shouted. "I don't deserve that!" he said pounding his prothesis with his other arm.

"Now, now gentlemen. Calm down. That is my decision and of course you are all free to appeal it to a higher court."

Mr. Freeman and Mr. Hopkins began a hushed conversation as the Judge stood up and began to leave the courtroom. Mr. Freeman approached Aimi and Saburo who were still sitting at the table dumbfounded at what had just happened. He offered his hand awkwardly to Saburo, not really sure how Saburo wanted to shake hands.

"Mr. Hopkins is willing to accept this settlement. I can work out the terms of payment with you if you like."

"Are you going to take his money?" Aimi pleaded.

Reluctantly Saburo said, "Yes. Look at me Aimi. I just don't have the heart to struggle with taking up farming again."

Disappointment dripped from her words as she asked," So what are you going to do with the money? By rights half of it is Eiji's"

"I am going to put it to my tuition fund as I go to college." Saburo said. "I don't think Eiji will mind and if he does, I'll pay him his half when I get a good job."

"What do you want to study to become?" Aimi directed the conversation to something perhaps more positive as they stood up to get ready to leave.

"I think I'll become a lawyer," Saburo announced. "Maybe I can help other people get justice when justice seems fickle and elusive."

38

For weeks Eiji was beside himself with grief and revulsion over the killing of his family members. The image of their bodies laid out, some burned nearly beyond recognition and others shot to death, recurred repeatedly as nightmares. During the days it took all his concentration and self-control to continue to function. But even that was a huge struggle as he continued to witness the ongoing evisceration of the Okinawans. By the end of the campaign when the 77th Division was sent back to Cebu in the Philippines to prepare for the invasion of Japan, an estimated 300,000 had perished in the Okinawan hecatomb. Somewhere along the way, Eiji stood at the railing of the troop transport in silence and sadly tossed his cowboy hat into the ocean. He just did not feel like one of the "good guys" anymore and the hat reminded him how far he had fallen from the ideals of his youth.

Eiji was assigned to the headquarters detachment of General Andrew D. Bruce, the commander of the 77th. He reverted to doing mostly what he had done back in the days of Operation Vengeance and the Battle of the Philippine Sea. He happened to be on KP duty on August 14th when the news was broadcast over Armed Forces Radio, blaring in the kitchen, that Japan had surrendered. The instantaneous elation of the cooks and men in the mess hall was riotous. Eiji himself began banging pots and pans together like cymbals. Men danced around, jumped on tables, and rushed to the EM club or their billets to obtain any alcohol they could get their hands on. Having endured the slugfest of Okinawa and scheduled to be part of the anticipated bloodier invasion of Japan, Eiji and his comrades were ecstatic and relieved that they would not have to fight anymore.

The 77th landed in Japan in October 1945. Almost every day, Eiji found it difficult to breathe as he passed through burned-out districts and streets and saw ragged people, almost zombie-like, shuffling around trying to scavenge whatever they could to eat or trade. The most common structural building material for Japanese homes was basically wood and paper and the American bombing campaigns which included incendiary bombs had ignited infernos throughout Japan. The initial expectations for the occupation were that the Japanese civilians would assault the occupiers with an even greater fierce intensity than had been the case on Okinawa. But when a recording of the Emperor, the Voice of the Crane, announced over national radio at noon on August 15th that "we" had decided to endure the unendurable and suffer the insufferable and accept peace in order to lay the foundation of peace for all generations, the Japanese people and nation knew the war was over. They became, for the most part, docile in defeat.

Part of Eiji's duties and responsibilities was to facilitate the release of the political prisoners who were scattered around the 77th's occupation zone. This was done by order of the occupation authorities as a beginning step to the re-democratization of Japan. He remembered how the Japanese patriotic paranoia of the military leaders, while he was a student at the Tokyo University of Commerce, had swept up hundreds of suspected leftists or anyone who had merely questioned or criticized the authoritarianism of those times. Occasionally, he wondered whatever might have happened to his classmates and Toshio Sasaki in the ensuing years. Were they even alive? If so, had their views of politics and governance changed? He certainly hoped so on all accounts.

Another wholly unanticipated duty of his was to address the occasional difficulties of a GI falling in love with a Japanese woman and wanting to get married. The military, locked into the conviction that the Japanese would passionately hate Americans, failed to develop any policies or procedures for different passions – perhaps even genuine love. The procedure that evolved was that GIs had to gain the permission of their commanding officers for such unions. Many of those officers were prejudiced against the Japanese and were citizens of the many states in America that had anti-miscegenation laws. Eiji well knew that biracial marriages between Anglos and Asians in California were against the law dating all the way back to the 1850s as was common in most of the other western or southern states. Officers from those states would refuse permission for their soldiers to marry, claiming, among other things, that it would be illegal for such couples to return to discriminatory states.

Even in the case of sympathetic officers, Eiji was asked to plumb the true and genuine depths of the Japanese woman's love for her GI intended. There was always the suspicion that gold diggers were trying to improve their situation in a nation that was starving to death by linking themselves to an American cornucopia of food and material goods. Viewing the conditions on the ground, Eiji could not really blame any woman who might be so motivated. But the protective, even paternalistic perspectives of commanders sought to weed out nefarious nuptials. Often commanders wanted to personally interview the love-struck couples and Eiji would be called in to translate. Sometimes permission was granted. Sometimes not and Eiji knew of at least one sad instance of a couple committing suicide rather than spending the rest of their lives apart.

Because of the relative tameness of the occupation, it was determined that the 77th was not needed for security in occupied Japan. Again, the whole unit exploded with joy and celebration when it was announced in March 1946 that it was being inactivated and returned to the States. Its members had fulfilled their obligation of serving for the duration and therefore could separate from the service should they so desire. There was no hesitation on Eiji's part about separation.

"Hallelujah!" Eiji shouted mostly to himself. "We are going home!"

"Yep, soldier," said the captain. "It's finally over."

"I can't honestly say I am going to miss you, sir."

"Understood," the captain said. "What are you going to do when you get back?"

"I am not sure. I'm going to rejoin my family in Santa Monica and do my best to help them rebuild their lives," Eiji answered. "You forget, they spent nearly three years in our version of concentration camps and were pretty much wiped out by that."

"Well, judging by what you've done for the country, we were lucky to have citizens like you."

Eiji became somewhat wistful. "Yes, we've always loved America. Only America hasn't always loved us back."

Three weeks later as their transport ship cut its way through the early morning fog, the ship's cargo of veterans standing on deck caught the first flash of the sunrise glistening off the Golden Gate Bridge. A roar of cheers arose from the men, Eiji among them. His heart was jubilant. He was back in the States and on the last leg of his wanderings through war and worriment.

39

"How long have you been back?" the editor of *The Rafu Shimpo* asked lowering the newspaper he was reading and looking over his glasses at Eiji sitting on the other side of the desk.

"Not quite a week," Eiji answered.

"Wow, you are an eager beaver. Why not take some time off and relax after all you've been through?"

'I'd rather get to work doing something interesting and remunerative."

"Well, what makes you think you are qualified to work for a newspaper?"

"I am fluently bilingual. Have a university degree from an institution in Tokyo in business and commerce. Just recently I was a translator for the United States Army and spent a little time working in the occupation."

"Interesting, but what are your writing qualifications?"

"Working for the Army, I had to write hundreds of reports, summaries of translations, and intelligence analytical pieces. I had to be accurate and to the point in clear prose without embellishment or exaggeration which could cost people their lives if it misled them."

A "humm" escaped the editor as he was mulling over what Eiji said. However important the news was, he could not think of any instances where people's lives actually depended on what he put into *The Rafu Shimpo*. It was a small bilingual paper struggling to be reborn as the Japanese community of Los Angeles reconstituted itself.

"I assume you can type," the editor dug deeper.

"Of course," Eiji confirmed.

"How about sales work?"

"I am not sure what you mean," Eiji said.

"Can you and are you willing to do marketing and promotion of the paper?"

"Sure, I learned something about marketing at the Tokyo University of Commerce, though I have not had many opportunities to use those skills in the last ten years."

The editor picked up a pipe from an ashtray on his desk and fiddled with it for a minute and then light it. A few sizeable puffs later, he leaned forward towards Eiji and extended his hand.

"Ok, I'll hire you for $25 a week. You'll cover all the business news and any international news we get out of Japan. You can make an extra 1% commission on any advertisements you manage to sell. Does that sound okay to you?"

"Absolutely. I'll even dust around here and sweep the floor," Eiji said with genuine gratuitous excitement in his voice.

"Don't tempt me. We have the cleaning done by the widow of a former employee who needs the income. When can you start?"

"Would tomorrow be too soon?" Eiji said with a wry smile.

"So, I guess that means you are taking the afternoon off, eh?" the Editor returned serve with a little humor of his own.

Both men smiled, shook hands and Eiji virtually bounced out of the office to the street. He got a job which was his number one priority since leaving the service. It was good, decent, and honorable work. He would not get rich but then he would not get too dirty if he were careful.

Everyone back at the Takara compound, as it had evolved into after Morio and Yo had built three additional rooms to accommodate everyone, was delighted with Eiji's good fortune. All but Saburo had jobs and income. Saburo, with government checks, had buckled down and was racing through the two-year program at Santa Monica College courtesy of the GI Bill as quickly as possible. He had his sights on bigger things. Even Kiku was making a little bit of money baking taiyaki cakes and selling them sometimes at the ocean park district of Santa Monica and sometimes at the pier.

By November 1946 they all had established a pattern, pace, and groove for their lives that included regular instances of playful enjoyment and vivacity.

"Hey, you two, tomorrow night let's go celebrate Armistice Day at the Aragon Ballroom. I hear that Leo Carrillo is going to make an appearance." Aimi bounced a suggestion to Eiji and Saburo.

"Why would we want to go and see him? He was one of the louder voices calling for our removal from California." Eiji's voice dripped with indignation.

"Maybe we should just forgive and forget," Aimi suggested.

"I can neither forgive nor forget what happened to us," Saburo said dramatically raising his hook arm.

"Ok, then we'll go someplace else. After all, we have something to celebrate – Saburo just got admitted to Loyola Law School. Isn't that great!"

"Really," Eiji asked. "You did not tell me you were planning to go to law school. Besides you only have an associate degree – how could you get into a law school?"

"Well, it turns out that law schools can admit anyone they think can do the work and have a reasonable chance of passing the bar exam. I applied, had good references from my teachers at Santa Monica College and Aimi helped me write my "why I want to be a lawyer" essay. We attached a picture of me in uniform and applied."

"So, you showed off all your service medals as well as your missing arm, eh? Wasn't that a pity ploy?" Eiji asked.

"Call it what you want. The whole system has been stacked against us since we were born – what is the harm of trying to take advantage of anything that might help balance the scales a bit?" Saburo was a little testy in his self-defense.

"I guess so," Eiji admitted. He did not want to take away the rightful rejoicing at Saburo's admittance. He was sure he would make a great lawyer. He returned to the plan for celebrating.

"Why don't we just meet someplace after work and we'll decide what we feel like then," Aimi suggested.

"Sounds good to me, what about you, Eiji? Saburo assented.

"Yep, that'll be fine."

The next evening Eiji and Saburo were standing on the street corner waiting for Aimi to join them.

"That's great that you got into law school. Are you going to be able to afford it?" Eiji asked.

"I am just a provisional student. I'll have to prove myself. Still got some GI money left but they said that if I did well in my first semester, they might consider giving me a small returned veteran scholarship of $100 per year."

"That's not much, Saburo."

"I know but every little bit helps, and I hope to get through the program in two years."

"What kind of law are you interested in?"

"I haven't really decided yet. I just want to do something that contributes to justice." Saburo answered.

Just then they noticed two men in navy uniforms and one in his Marine finest walking towards that at a quick and perhaps menacing pace.

"Hey, you guys! Shouted one of them. "Japs, right?"

Before Eiji could offer much of an answer they had already come within arm's length, and they surrounded them as if they were ready for some sort of physical confrontation.

"We're out here celebrating Armistice Day and what better way to do so than to bash a few dirty Japs," said the Marine.

"Now hold on fellows," Saburo said putting up his arms defensively to fend them off if he had to. Eiji took a position at his back and surveyed the angry faces of two burly navy guys closing the circle.

"What did you guys do during the war – spy for Tojo?" asked one of them.

"Wait a minute, gentlemen. You've got this all wrong." Eiji began to ply diplomacy as one of the fellows shoved him a bit back into Saburo.

"Hey single wing?" started the Marine staring him right in the eye. "What's your story?"

"Look we are not in our uniforms right now, but we served too, just like you guys," protested Eiji.

"Liars," said the third navy veteran.

"No, it's true. Saburo here served in the 100th/442nd in Italy and France. He helped rescue the Lost Battalion. Ever heard of that?"

"In fact, part of me is probably still there," Saburo said raising his right arm.

"Is that so?" said the Marine. "I heard of that – that was some bloodbath." He said with a tone of grudging respect in his voice.

Saburo just nodded his head as he stepped back from the Marine.

"What about you skinny," a navy fellow motioned towards Eiji. "You seem to have all your body parts. What did you do?"

"I did translation work out of Macarthur's headquarters," Eiji said straightening his sport coat from the ruffle the previous shove raised.

"Big deal," the more aggressive and suspicious navy vet said.

"Yeah, I helped piece together the information that made Operation Vengeance and the killing of Admiral Yamamoto possible."

"Really?" another navy fellow said slowly nodding his head.

"And later, I helped sort out the Japanese battle plan which led to the victory at the Battle of the Philippine Sea."

"You mean the Marianas Turkey Shoot?" gasped the third navy guy. "Wow, I was on the Lexington and those pilots came back claiming that the whole thing was just like a Turkey Shoot!"

"Yep, I did my part behind the scenes trying to set up the ducks, or as you suggest the turkeys, for you guys to shoot."

Eiji did not want to mention his more agonizing experiences in the invasion of Okinawa. That was still very private and raw inside him. He and Saburo offered enough to establish a veteran's rapport with fellow warriors.

"Well, you two, you are alright," the Marine said slapping Saburo on the back. "Sorry to be so rough with you guys. It's just we all lost plenty of pals to those Jap, I mean Japanese, fighters. Seeing you triggered those memories."

"I get it," Eiji said.

"Hey, can we buy you guys a couple of beers? We can swap stories, true and otherwise."

"No thanks, fellows. We have other plans. We are waiting for my sister to join us. But thanks anyway."

"Alright then." Take care of yourselves, the Marine said as he clasped Saburo's right hook in both of his hands and shook "hands" with him.

"We all did our part in our own way," Eiji said as the men began to move off.

"Whew," Saburo said. "I was afraid that was going to turn into some sort of rumble."

"Yeah, a pretty close call," Eiji said taking out a cigarette and lighting it up to take the edge off his impatience over Aimi's tardiness.

"But if it came to that, I do not think they would not have wanted to tussle with this," Saburo said holding up his right arm. "I could rip them up with this."

They impatiently walked around in circles under the streetlight looking at their watches.

"Where could she be?" asked Saburo.

"She's coming from work in Boyle Heights. Probably missed her bus." Eiji reasoned.

Suddenly they heard a sharp scream and a woman's voice pitifully pleading for help. Instantly they knew it was Aimi. They looked down the street in the direction of her compellingly painful outcries from around the corner. They began to run down the street as fast as possible. When they rounded the corner, they saw six or seven thuggish hooligans surrounding her and assaulting her. They had ripped her nurse's uniform exposing her brassier and breast. One of them was trying to lift her dress and several were taunting her. A knife was in the hands of the man lording over her telling her to take off her clothes.

Both Eiji and Saburo lunged into the crowd and tackled the two men closest to Aimi. Eiji was desperately wrestling with one of the assailants and Saburo managed to regain his feet and took a defensive stand shielding Aimi as best he could. Eiji and his opponent stood each other up and Eiji also assumed a protective position near Aimi.

"Ah, lucky us," one of the men said. "We get to beat up a couple of Japs and have their woman as well. What a night."

Aimi was crying and doing her best to reposition her torn blouse to cover her exposed skin.

"Leave us alone," she shouted. "Just go away."

"Why would we do that?" asked one of the brutes. "We are just about to have some fun here."

The sound of two switchblades snapping into position made Eiji and Saburo realize that they were in a very dangerous situation.

"There's just two of you and six of us, pal," the seeming leader of the pack said. "I don't think the odds are in your favor," he continued chuckling a bit.

"Well, maybe this will even up the odds a bit," they heard the voice of the Marine from behind the ruffians. He and his mates had continued to meander through the streets and also heard Aimi's cries. They had sprinted to the scene as well.

The gang members repositioned themselves each singling out one of the navy men, the Marine, Eiji and Saburo. It was going to be six on six, and doubts were forming in the heads of the goons.

In a flash, the one closest to Saburo lunged at him with his knife. Saburo deftly stepped to the side and slashed him deeply across his face with his right hook. He let out a scream of pain and dropped his knife as he clutched the gaping wound. Blood streamed through his fingers and started dripping on the ground.

Seeing that, the rest of the punks looked at each other and then hightailed it, scattering in different directions. The wounded man began to walk away as quickly as he could.

"You better get that looked at," Aimi threw at him in an ironic tone. "That looks like it might be serious."

They stood Aimi up. Eiji offered her his coat and the Marine took off one of his campaign ribbons to use it as a pin to fix her blouse more modestly.

"Glad you guys showed up. It looked touch and go for a minute or two." Eiji said.

"Yeah, just like the Vosges Mountains again," Saburo said trying to wipe the blood off his hook with a handkerchief. "Thanks, guys, thanks a lot. What can we do to show our appreciation?"

The Marine stepped forward and admiringly took Saburo's blood dripping right hand. "How about having that beer with us now?"

Eiji looked at Aimi who had remarkably regained most of her composure.

"Sure! You got it!"

40

Two years had passed since the "battle of Armistice Day. The three of them elected to go out and celebrate another milestone for Saburo – he passed the bar exam. In the afternoon while at the newspaper office, Eiji reflected on things. He remembered how pitiful and helpless Aimi first looked that night on the ground and facing probable rape or worse. He also remembered the terrible pictures from his friend Toshiro Sasaki's brother of the women in Nanking. He just shook his head at the incomprehensible cruelty that humans could rent upon other humans.

Aimi and Saburo were at Boardners bar for another celebration. By 1948 it was no longer so necessary for Saburo to trade on how and why he lost his arm fighting the Nazis in Europe in order to get admittance to places. Still, they were seated in the rear mostly out of sight and began to enjoy their drinks and the music.

"You passed the bar exam!" Aimi let out with a peel of laughter and congratulations.

"Yep, I did, didn't I?" Saburo said obviously pleased with himself and raising his beer to Aimi for a toast.

"Well, what are you going to do now?" she asked.

"I've been thinking it over. There is this guy, Wayne Collins, who has been filing all sorts of lawsuits in federal courts about the unconstitutionality of the relocation process to try to regain some justice if not redress for what was done to us. I hear he even wants to challenge the legality of the Renunciation Act and the forced repatriation of at least the Nisei to Japan. I am hoping I can join his legal team."

"Oh, that would be great!" Aimi said enthusiastically.

"That reminds me I just got a letter from Nomo, long-delayed, about her situation. It is terrible."

At that point, Eiji appeared carrying a bag with something in it. He slipped into a chair and put the bag under the table.

"Eiji! You made it." Saburo greeted him.

"I had to close down some things at the newspaper before I could get here. Sorry I am late."

"No problem," Aimi said obviously in good cheer. "We are just honoring Saburo's victory over the Bar Exam. He's a lawyer now!"

"That's great!" Eiji contributed to the celebratory mood. The waitress came and Eiji ordered a beer for himself and another round for Aimi and Saburo.

"I was just telling Aimi that I am hoping to link up with this Wayne Collins guy in his legal work against the government about relocation."

"I've heard about what he's doing. He is trying to get the whole thing overturned on constitutional grounds. Pretty much the whole Japanese American community is pulling for him."

"Collins is even trying to get the forced repatriation of American citizens to Japan overturned," Aimi said.

"And Aimi was just about to tell me what has happened to Nomo and her family after they were sent back. You never knew Nomo, but she was a sweet kid and a thoroughgoing American."

"True and her letter details the tragedies that they have endured since their expulsion."

"Right but it was of their own volition." Saburo chimed in.

"Not really, her father forced her into it. Be that as it may, the Nakamuras had no relatives of any kind left in Japan. They became homeless refugees immediately. Her father subsequently died of a heart attack – probably due to all the pressure and stress they went through."

"You saw some of the conditions in the early days after the war, Eiji. Things have only gotten worse."

"I can imagine."

"Nomo hates it. They live in a cardboard box on the street. The only income they have is from Nomo working in a dance hall charging GIs a few yen for dances. She has to constantly fend off their more disgusting advances and suggestions."

"God," Saburo said.

Suddenly a reasonably well-dressed man pushed his way through the crowd and accosted them.

"You're Japanese aren't you." the man said with hostility practically foaming on his lips.

"Actually, we are Americans," Saburo replied instantly.

"Don't get cute with me crip. You know what I mean."

"We are actually of Okinawan descent," Eiji said trying a diversionary tactic.

"I ought to beat you bloody, right now," the man said brandishing his fists.

"Why?" Aimi asked.

"My uncle and his family were taken to a Japanese concentration camp in Shandong, China, and held there for three years. They almost starved and were repeatedly mistreated. Their only crime was being Americans."

"How ironic," Eiji said. "The same thing happened to our families too."

The man was nonplussed. "What?"

"Yeah, almost three years at Heart Mountain concentration camp in Montana was no picnic for me or my mother and father, either," Aimi said.

"Maybe we did not have it as bad as your uncle's family, and we are sorry for that, but I hated Heart Mountain so much I volunteered for the army and collected some German-made lead in a French forest," Saburo said.

"And our crime was the same as your uncle's – we were Americans."

Dazed a bit, the offensive assailant did his best to gracefully withdraw.

"Back to Nomo's situation. We've got to do something." Aimi insisted.

"That's my plan. I want to go to Japan and see what I can do to extract her and Chu from the iron maiden of their situation." Saburo announced.

"What?" Eiji asked. "How are you going to do that?"

"I'll appeal to anyone and everyone's sense of justice. Maybe as a lawyer, I can intimidate or fool somebody to take heed of the Constitution and the human rights of American citizens. And I want you to help me."

"Me? What can I do?"

"You know Japan, your language skills are better than mine. And you had some initial experience with the occupation authorities. You might even know somebody back there." Saburo appealed to his best friend.

Eiji thought it over. He had fallen into a comfortable routine at the newspaper and living at home with the family. Bit increasingly it was less and less fulfilling for him. He wanted to do something more directly positively impacted people's lives.

"Ok, I'll do it on one condition."

"What's that?"

"That after we are done doing whatever we can for Nomo, you help me settle the situation for our "cousin" Mirai. You two never met her but she is also a sweet girl with nobody to take care of her. We ought to try to bring her here to the states and be her family."

Aimi and Saburo looked at each other and began nodding their heads. "Sure, why not?" Aimi said.

"Oh, that reminds me, Saburo, I brought something here to commemorate your passing of the bar exam." Eiji reached under the table and produced the bag he had with him when he first arrived. Reaching in the bag he pulled out a brand-new beautiful cowboy hat and handed it to Saburo.

"If we are going to ride off into the sunset to save Nomo, you better wear the uniform," Eiji laughed. "Just like the old days, right?"

Aimi giggled but Saburo broke out in almost uncontrollable laughter.

"What's so funny?" Eiji asked.

"Well, hoping that I would be able to recruit you to help me joust at some windmills," Saburo began as he reached under the table too. "I thought this might be appropriate." He handed Eiji a similar brand-new white cowboy hat. They both put them on looking into each other's eyes amidst their rolling laughter.

Eiji adjusted his hat and quickly switched into his impersonation of Harry Truman. He had memorized a portion of Truman's speech in July 1946 awarding the Presidential Unit citation to the 442nd.

"I think it was my predecessor who said that Americanism is not a matter of race or creed, it is a matter of the heart... You fought not only the enemy, but you fought prejudice — and you have won. Keep up that fight, and we will continue to win — to make this great Republic stand for just what the Constitution says it stands for the welfare of all the people all the time."

"Maybe we can transform some of the uniformly undeserved loathing we've endured these many years into some wholly warranted welcoming," Saburo added.

"Maybe, maybe," Aimi said as they all clicked their glasses and sipped their beer.

COVER PHOTOS CREDITS

Upper left:
https://commons.wikimedia.org/wiki/File:Bundesarchiv_Bild_183-1983-0422-312,_Umsiedler_auf_dem_G%C3%BCterbahnhof_Berlin-Pankow.jpg

Below to the right:
https://en.wikipedia.org/wiki/Military_Intelligence_Service_(United_States)#/media/File:MIS_Language_School.jpg

Bottom:
https://en.wikipedia.org/wiki/442nd_Infantry_Regiment_(United_States)#/media/File:442_regimental_combat_team.jpg.

ABOUT THE AUTHOR

Introducing the author who transformed his lifelong fascination with China and Asia into gripping historical fiction. With a Ph.D. in Chinese history and American Diplomatic History, he spent years as a Foreign Expert in Beijing before becoming a cherished professor in California. Now, in retirement, he's devoting himself to his lifelong passion of writing novels. Get lost in his captivating tales, including *A Thousand Crane, Uniformly Undeserved*, and *Ashes and Memories*, and be on the lookout for his upcoming trilogy about an American family in China. Don't miss out on the chance to discover a master storyteller.

OTHER BOOKS BY THIS AUTHOR

Quiet Passages: The Exchange of Civilians Between the United States and Japan During the Second World War

In 1939 the U.S. Department of State created the Special Division to handle some of the problems that the complexity of modern warfare had created for diplomatic means. During the Second World War, those duties came to include the implementation of civilian personnel exchanges between the 'arsenal of democracy' and the Axis nations. Quiet Passages is the study of the role in carrying out such exchanges with the Japanese government, which was more complex than the exchanges conducted with Germany and Italy. The study is based on records and files of the Special Division, corroborated as needed by other sources.

U.S. History

U.S. History is designed to meet the scope and sequence requirements of most introductory courses. The text provides a balanced approach to U.S. history, considering the people, events, and ideas that have shaped the United States from both the top down (politics, economics, diplomacy) and bottom up (eyewitness accounts, lived experience). U.S. History covers key forces that form the American experience, with particular attention to issues of race, class, and gender.

A Thousand Cranes

Love, hate, and memories are the drivers that propel us through life's confusing mazes and narrowly missed collisions with others that can change the arc of our fates. A Thousand Cranes tackles some of the issues of the often hidden and lingering effects of the Vietnam war on men struggling to construct useful civilian lives after surviving the uncivil life of that conflict. For college professors like Roland and Alex, or campus cop Butch, not even the relative calm and structure of academic life in a small Southern California college can fully ease the abiding terrors of their Vietnam years. Is it even possible to simply think your way out of deep emotional trauma? Is the presence of loving family and friends enough to quiet the disturbing voices in the back of the mind? If higher education cannot cure the more deeply embedded dysfunctions of good men, then what is its purpose? And, above all, what are the effects of their problems on the people they love and who care about them? Tracking the stories of third-generation immigrants with roots in Eastern Europe, this novel casts a wide net in examining its characters' disparate, but ultimately related, sagas. It is a large world, but the basic human drama of survival and the larger challenge of how to form a caring environment for the planet's caretakers is indeed a shared experience, as the characters in this rewarding book discover.

Ashes and Memories

The fusion of physical and interpersonal crises sometimes triggers the need to make unanticipated and difficult choices in life. When 70-year-old widower Fred Korman suffers a stroke during a long-distance run, his life takes an unexpected turn. As he struggles to recover, he faces a new challenge, protecting his best friend Susan from her abusive ex-husband Tony. But when Tony starts to threaten Fred and his family, Fred must find a way to end the harassment for good. Meanwhile, Fred's son Aaron is starting a new career and dealing with the news that his girlfriend is pregnant. With pressure mounting from all sides, Fred must summon all his strength and wit to protect his loved ones and find a way forward. This gripping novel explores the power of love, friendship, and determination in the face of adversity.